Never a Stranger
Patricia Wilson

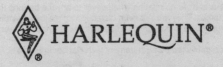

HARLEQUIN®

TORONTO • NEW YORK • LONDON
AMSTERDAM • PARIS • SYDNEY • HAMBURG
STOCKHOLM • ATHENS • TOKYO • MILAN • MADRID
PRAGUE • WARSAW • BUDAPEST • AUCKLAND

ISBN 0-373-17387-3

NEVER A STRANGER

First North American Publication 1998.

Copyright © 1995 by Patricia Wilson.

This edition published by arrangement with Harlequin Books S.A.

® and TM are trademarks of the publisher. Trademarks indicated with ® are registered in the United States Patent and Trademark Office, the Canadian Trade Marks Office and in other countries.

Printed in U.S.A.

CHAPTER ONE

'I WON'T! I will not! Do you understand me, Selina?' Kirsty glared at the phone, furious that her stepmother was not there to see her angry face.

'I can hardly fail to understand. Your words are quite specific,' Selina Sinclair replied, her voice brittle with annoyance. 'However, I feel you owe this to your father, and it's little enough to ask after all the years of love and care he lavished on you. We're asking you to give up a couple of weeks, nothing more.'

'No, *you're* asking me!' Kirsty corrected sharply. 'If my father really wanted me there, he'd be phoning himself and not leaving it to you. As to the years of loving care, they were before your time. I suggest you give up your trip to Paris and repay the years of care he's lavished on you—to say nothing of the money!'

Kirsty slammed the phone down and sank to the nearest chair. Her legs were shaking, so were her hands. She was not given to violent conversations or violent disagreements. Any conversation with Selina upset her for days, but she had to make a stand because Selina never gave up. It had been like that from the first. The difference now was that Selina was no longer dealing with a child, she was dealing with a grown woman, a successful woman of twenty-four.

She stared at the ceiling frustratedly and then got up to make a hot drink, another throw-back to the past. After any sort of stressful encounter she had always craved a hot drink and the realisation made her angrier than ever. She could hardly say she had fully escaped until the thought of Selina washed right over her and caused no ripple in her life.

And she knew perfectly well who would be going to Paris with Selina. The darkly guarded secret was no secret to her. She could just picture the scene, and the picture was all too vivid: Selina's brilliantly blonde head and a dark head next to it—blue-black hair—and slate-grey eyes that would look into the baby-blue of Selina's and smile. Kirsty clenched her teeth and poured boiling water into the cup. Adam Frazer would be right there at the airport, tall, handsome and treacherous.

Or would they meet in Paris? He was a little too well-known to risk meeting Selina right out in the open. He had too much to lose, and so had Selina for that matter. If her father ever found out it would kill him, but she knew he never would find out; they were too clever. After all, they had had plenty of practice. This affair had been going on for years—seven years to her certain knowledge.

Kirsty took her drink and walked down the shining wooden steps to the gallery, fighting to calm her burst of rage and trying to sweep the past away, although the mental images of those two together were too strong to cast aside entirely. The gallery was empty at that moment, and she was grateful. Glaring at prospective buyers was not exactly good business practice. The last of the rage drained away as she gazed round the long, well-lit room that housed her collection. It was satisfying to know that she had done well, and even though a deep sadness still lingered at the back of her mind Kirsty fought it off.

She was a success. Her little business flourished. Even among the big galleries she had made a place for herself because she had specialised. Every painting in the place was of an animal, and people came from far away to browse among the horses, dogs and cats that were lovingly presented in glowing oils on the gallery walls.

Kirsty had quite a few American clients and she was now often asked to search for something specific. Her latest American customer was collecting setters, and last week she had found her another one, an Old English setter. She had bought it at a sale for a very low price, keeping her glee well-contained until the hammer finally fell. She smiled now when she remembered the auctioneer's caustically raised brows as she had outbid the few people who were interested. He had known the value of the painting, and he had also known that she would make a good profit. Most of the auctioneers knew her now, and the fame of her little gallery was spreading like a prairie fire. Not bad for someone who had given up her course at college because she had been just too unhappy to continue.

Susan came through from the back, putting her coat on, her glance intensifying as she noticed Kirsty's face.

'Trouble?' she asked astutely, but Kirsty shook her head and smiled.

'Not really. It's just that I think I'll have to go home soon, maybe for a couple of weeks.' Susan had worked for her in the gallery for quite a while now, and in many ways she was a friend, but there were some things that even a friend should not know.

The last thought wiped the smile from Kirsty's lips and she glanced at her watch.

'You get off, Susan. I'll close up. It's just about time.'

'Anything you want me to do, just ask,' Susan said with another sharp glance at Kirsty's face, and Kirsty nodded, but it was all a formality and she knew it. No amount of help would wipe out the past and the knowledge she had kept hidden for years.

As Susan left Kirsty let down the window-blinds and locked the doors. She wished now that she had agreed to go out tonight with Guy. She had been looking forward to an evening alone before Selina's call. Now she was fighting to keep the bitterness away, fighting to cast off the pictures that raced into her head.

Upstairs in her flat, she just gave up trying. The thought of going back home, of *having* to go back home, was too much to bear. She had not been back since she was nineteen. Oh, she had seen her father. He called in to see her quite often—in fact, she was collecting paintings of shire-horses for him right now. But home! She would never go back. She couldn't—not with Selina and the thought of Adam. Their guilty relationship had washed off on her, making her feel the guilt too. In her old surroundings she would not be able to pretend, and one day she would explode with her knowledge, maybe even in front of her father.

Not that Adam Frazer was there now. He had a wonderful place of his own, or so her father had informed her proudly. He still adored Adam—hadn't they both at one time? She couldn't take that joy and pride away from her father, couldn't tell him that his wonderful protégé and partner was having a long-time adulterous affair with his wife.

She had longed to blurt it out when she was still in her teens, had longed to see the superior smile die on Selina's beautiful face, but always her love for her father had kept her silent. Truth to tell, Adam's grey eyes had kept her silent too, because when he had looked at her she had never really been able to believe it all. It was true, though—hadn't he as good as admitted it?

Kirsty made herself a light meal and afterwards sat down to watch television. She hardly ever did that, and tonight she had been going to wash her hair. Somehow, though, she couldn't summon up the energy. The pictures stayed in her mind, and finally she stared at the set with unseeing eyes as her mind returned to the time when everything had changed.

She had always been a shy child but her life had been one of complete happiness. Her father was a wealthy businessman and she had attended a school close to home, taken and brought back every day by her mother. They had been alike in everything, always delighted to see each other, both secure and content in the love that had been poured on them. Donald Sinclair had spent every spare minute with his family, and Kirsty's early memories were of racing to meet her father as he came in each evening, her mother close behind her, and of the hugging, the laughter and the warm feeling of all being together again after a day apart.

Their beautiful world had been shattered when her mother was killed in a car accident. Kirsty had been eleven years old and very vulnerable, trying to cope with her own grief and comfort her father. Nothing had been the same but gradually, over a couple of years, they had settled into a sort of numbing recovery. That was when she had first seen Adam Frazer. He had been new to her father's firm, straight from university, and she had understood from the talk she'd heard that he was brilliant.

Kirsty was thirteen, still at the same local private school, and it added a touch of interest to her life that Adam was frequently invited to lunch at the weekends. Her father was greatly impressed by the financial genius of someone so young. They seemed to spend hours walking round the garden in deep discussion, and Kirsty never felt left out. There was something special about this man with blue-black hair and slate-grey eyes. They were eyes that saw a great deal, and somehow she felt he knew exactly how she still grieved.

Her tentative smiles were always returned, and finally he became just 'Adam'. Her face was gloomy if he failed to spend some part of each weekend with them. She was slowly recovering from the blow of losing her mother, but deep inside she felt guilt that she should begin to live again when her father could not, so it was with an astonishment close to panic that she learned he was marrying again.

Kirsty could not battle with her conflicting feelings. She was recovering, so why should he not recover too? But the thought of another woman taking her mother's place was more than she could bear. On the day he told her she went off by herself, missed the lunch she had been looking forward to and missed Adam. She knew she could not sit at the table and be normal, and she had no wish to hurt her father.

It was Adam who found her, and even now she could still see him coming down to the river that ran close to the grounds of Parbury Hall. She could still see the way he simply sat beside her and looked out across the water, his grey eyes narrowed against the sunlight.

'He's only forty-four, Kirsty,' he reminded her quietly. 'He's still a young man. You can't expect him to live like a hermit for the rest of his life.'

'I thought he loved my mother,' Kirsty said heartbrokenly, and he turned her tearstained face to his.

'Never doubt that,' he said softly. 'From what I gather, his whole life was wrapped up in you and your mother.

It was two years ago. People mourn and then recover. You are recovering.'

The grey eyes looked into hers and Kirsty could not lie. She *was* recovering, slowly but surely.

'Yes, but he was married to her.'

'And you loved her just as much, in a different way.'

Kirsty nodded miserably, and his arm came round her slim shoulders as he gave her a hug.

'You'll survive, Kirsty Sinclair.'

When Adam said it, it seemed possible, and she tried. She tried very hard. But with Selina it soon became clear that it was fight or go under, and for a while Kirsty went under, because Selina was a glamorous, grasping woman who disliked the competition of a young girl in the house, and she was clever. At thirteen, Kirsty was no match for a beautiful twenty-nine-year-old woman who knew exactly where she was going.

There was discord, minor arguments that left Kirsty unable to explain things to her father, and he became more and more frustrated, easily convinced that she was merely showing the sometimes unbearable behaviour of an adolescent. Minor arguments grew into major ones, and Kirsty was packed off to boarding-school before the year was out. Selina was left with a clear field and Kirsty was too shy, too hurt and withdrawn, to cope very well. She became isolated, her life deeply unhappy.

Adam was the only brightness in her life. She seemed to be taken under his wing. Holidays at home were only bearable because he was often there. He took her out on jaunts with him and ignored Selina's raised eyebrows and sarcastic comments. He sometimes came to school to see her and take her out to tea, and by the time she was fifteen he was her very best friend, even though he was twenty-six and years older. It seemed to Kirsty that, whatever happened, Adam would save her. It was like possessing her very own knight in shining armour. As she grew further away from her father she grew closer to Adam, and because of him she could face Selina when she was at home. He gave her stability, almost something to live for, and she rebuilt her life around him.

Kirsty would never forget the summer that things fell apart. For once, she invited a friend home with her. Karen Swift was the daughter of an army officer and that year she had been faced with staying for most of the summer holiday at school or visiting relatives she disliked. She came home with Kirsty because, although Kirsty didn't want to share Adam with anybody, she couldn't bear to think of Karen staying in school.

Adam was surprised too. Already he was her hero, closer to her than her own father, and now she was seventeen she saw how handsome he was, how that slow smile changed his face, how the grey eyes could look into hers and bring a soft flush to her cheeks. Kirsty had never felt quite like this about him before, and although it meant that she was not so completely comfortable with him as she had been as a child, the new feelings were exciting and very precious.

On her first morning back, Kirsty was up long before Karen and Adam caught up with her as she walked in the grounds.

'You brought reinforcements with you,' he chastised softly as he drew level with her. 'It never occurred to me that I might have to share you with somebody else this holiday.'

Kirsty blushed and looked away, not quite knowing how much he was teasing.

'Karen had nowhere to go,' she began. 'I couldn't just leave her at school, and I didn't think you would mind.'

'I don't mind, angel,' he assured her with a smile. He caught her hand and looked down at her intently, his eyes skimming her flushed cheeks. 'It was probably a good idea. Safety in numbers.'

'I'm safe with you,' Kirsty protested, and his eyes held hers for much longer than usual before he turned her back towards the garden and her walk.

'Well, you always have been,' he murmured. He said nothing else for a while, just walked with her as he always had done, and gradually Kirsty's heartbeats slowed to normal.

It was only as they were coming back towards the house that he brought up the subject of school again.

'How much longer do you have to stay in that damned place?' he suddenly asked harshly.

'School? Another year.' Kirsty looked at him a bit anxiously. He seemed annoyed, tense, and her anxiety was not lessened when he turned to her impatiently.

'Another year? Hell!'

When she went on looking at him warily his face relaxed, darkened, and he reached for her hand, turning her fingers in his and glancing up at her from beneath dark brows.

'Does it seem a long time to you, Kirsty, or am I being just too impatient?'

'It—it seems a long time,' she agreed, and he smiled and touched her cheek gently. For a moment he seemed to be very close, and Kirsty found it hard to breathe, and then he grinned at her, the old Adam she knew so well.

'When we go out this holiday we'll take Karen,' he assured her softly. 'Sharing the time with her might be a very good idea.'

And she knew what he meant. She wasn't stupid.
Things had subtly changed for her over the time she had
known him. Now they had changed for Adam, and she
hugged the secret to herself, glowing with it, thrilled by
it.

It was a beautiful, wistful holiday, and even Selina
didn't manage to spoil it. Karen didn't notice how Adam
looked at Kirsty. She didn't notice how often his hand
came to Kirsty's arm, how he lifted her down so carefully when they were out walking and any fence had to
be climbed, and Kirsty wanted to linger close to him,
make the most of every moment. He knew too. His eyes
smiled into hers and she understood only too well that
Karen was an unsuspecting chaperon.

Towards the end of the holiday her father made an
announcement that altered everything. He waited until
the last minute at dinner and then told all of them that
Adam was to have a full partnership in the firm.

'I can't do with having a financial wizard escape,'
Donald Sinclair said. 'As a partner, he won't wish to
move on. I know perfectly well that a few firms have
been snapping at his heels. Now we've got him, safe and
sound.'

Of course, Adam had already known and he had just
smiled quietly, but Kirsty had been overwhelmed with
joy. It meant that he would never go. Now she had him
forever. She would never be parted from Adam.

It was then she realised that Adam was not looking
at her. His eyes were locked with the baby-blue eyes of
Selina, and Kirsty's own smile faded as she watched.
Something passed between them, and her skin suddenly
felt cold. She glanced at her father, but he was busily
pouring more wine, unaware that any atmosphere had

grown, and when Kirsty looked back Selina had her emotions on the usual tight rein.

It was too late, though. Kirsty had seen the look in her eyes and had seen a sort of triumph in Adam's eyes too. When he looked at her then, Kirsty could not smile back. She felt as if she was standing on a lift that was going down very fast, shattering her life as it went.

That night, she couldn't sleep. There was a veranda to her room and she stood there thinking, the lights out and only the light of the moon to allow her to see. It was warm, with a soft breeze blowing. She drew back rapidly as she suddenly heard voices down below.

'So, you've got what you want, finally?' It was Selina's voice, and even before she heard him Kirsty knew that the next voice would belong to Adam.

'Not entirely. However, I'm on my way. I know exactly what I want. I have done for a long time.'

'Things will stay exactly as they are while Donald is alive,' Selina assured him, with a soft, seductive laugh.

'I don't see why they should,' Adam countered smoothly. 'After all, they haven't stayed as they supposedly are so far, have they? Donald hasn't the faintest idea of the things that go on around him. He's a very trusting man.'

'Lucky for both of us,' Selina remarked. 'Are you going to do anything about all this?'

'Not right away. I can wait. I've already waited for three years.'

'So you're going to continue playing me along?' Selina asked in a soft voice, and Kirsty heard Adam's low laugh. It almost sounded cruel.

'Why not? You like being played along, Selina. It's part of the excitement. You love to see how far this can go without Donald finding out.'

Kirsty heard no more. She stepped quietly into her room and silently closed the windows. She had already heard more than she wanted to hear. Her instincts at dinner had been all too correct. Adam Frazer was having an affair with her stepmother, right under her father's nose, and her father had now given Adam a good deal of power. He was a full partner. If he should decide to go off with Selina, there was nothing her father could do about it.

The secret dreams she had cherished for herself fell to dust. She was seventeen, not even old enough to matter, and nothing to Adam when a woman like Selina was there. Anything she had felt between herself and Adam this holiday was just her imagination.

Next morning her suspicions were more than confirmed. When Karen came down to breakfast she looked a little stunned, and couldn't wait to get Kirsty by herself.

'I can hardly believe it,' she whispered. 'Last night your stepmother and Adam were billing and cooing.'

'Don't be ridiculous!' Instantly Kirsty jumped on the defensive, but she didn't doubt the words of her friend.

'Well, believe me or not,' Karen said huffily. 'I had my window open and I heard them. I couldn't see, but you don't have to see, do you?' She gave Kirsty a pitying look and then never mentioned it again.

After that, Kirsty dropped Adam flat, and if she hadn't known better she would have been tricked into believing that he found it hurtful. Not that he had ever spent a great deal of time with her. He was too busy working, travelling all over the world for the firm and handling the business affairs of a company that had simply grown with the years.

What had begun in her grandfather's day as a building firm was now a worldwide company, dealing with all types of things from building airports to computers. Adam was at the very heart of things and always had been. Now, though, he had his hands firmly on the reins, and he was not the sort of person to let anything slip.

When he looked at her now, she looked away; when he seemed to be about to approach her, she found some reason to go in the opposite direction, and although it hurt, it did not hurt as much as his betrayal. When she returned to school she made sure she always knew when he would visit her, and she joined several clubs that did not particularly interest her but gave her a very good excuse to be unavailable if he should arrive.

He took it all in his stride during the next year, until she refused to go to university and opted for art school, getting herself a flat in London and never going home. And it was on her nineteenth birthday that Adam finally tracked her down to her newly acquired lair. He came completely unannounced and there was no escape. She had no alternative but to invite him in, and he stood looking round, with a frown on his face that promised trouble.

'Is this how you intend to live your life?' He looked at the general chaos that overflowed in every direction. 'You're going to art school to fritter away your time and then coming back here at night to live in this squalor?'

'I am not living in squalor,' Kirsty demurred. She was still young enough to be unsure of herself, still too raw to take this sort of tongue-lashing and give back as good as she got. 'I've only just moved in. When I'm sorted out——'

'And when will that be, Kirsty—when you're about thirty? You have a good brain but you are not an artist. God knows how you got into this school!'

'I can draw!' Kirsty protested, and he turned away impatiently.

'Plenty of people can draw, but it doesn't make them capable of earning their living or even being satisfied with their ability. You know damned well you should have been at university.'

'It's none of your business!' Kirsty reminded him loudly, and he spun round and grasped her arms.

'It never has been any of my business, but you've never objected to my advice or my proximity before.' He stared at her unswervingly. 'So what happened, Kirsty? Why am I suddenly unacceptable? Why did my presence become so distasteful to you?'

'I'm nineteen. I've grown up!'

'Have you?' He let her go and looked at her scathingly. 'You seemed to me to be more grown-up when you were thirteen. At least then you were not a churlish female with ungrateful tendencies. You had the ability to work things out too.'

'The ability grew!' Kirsty snapped, stung into anger by his assertion that she was churlish. 'I've worked things out very well. I know just what you are now. I'm not as easily taken in as when I was a child.'

His hands seemed to leap out at her, and before she could move Kirsty found herself once more grasped by the biting steel of his fingers.

'And what am I?' he grated, his eyes as cold and grey as the sea. 'What have you turned me into that you never come back home and never wish to see me?'

Even then she could not actually make herself say the words. She could not force her tongue to utter what was eating into her mind. How could she say that she knew he was having an affair with Selina? It would finally break some unseen bond that she was even now loath to break.

'I just don't like you any more,' she said stiffly, and for a second the grey eyes seemed to turn to ice.

She was mesmerised. Always those eyes had smiled at her, softly grey, comforting, warm, but now they seemed to have no colour, no feeling, as if some light behind them had gone out. She was glad she had not spoken out, because there was something about him that told her he would possibly have killed her. For a second, Adam didn't seem to be there at all.

He let her go and turned away, staring out of the window—a window that did not yet have curtains.

'Maybe you did grow up after all,' he murmured. 'I imagine that little girls like just about anyone who is kind to them. Foolish of me to expect it to continue. Obviously you've reached the age of discernment. Let's hope you choose your friends with acumen in future.'

He turned to leave, but Kirsty couldn't just let things go at that.

'Why?' she asked in an agonised voice. 'Why did you have to be like that?'

'Like what?' He looked at her disparagingly. 'As far as I can see, the condemned man isn't about to be told what crime he committed. Does it matter, in any case? You don't like me now that you've grown up. The choice is yours, Kirsty. I hope everything works out for you.'

She could see that he doubted it, and she walked about for a long time after he had gone, unable to settle to doing anything at all. She knew perfectly well that she should not be here. She knew perfectly well that she should be studying, making use of her brain in an entirely different way, but she also knew that she now had another unhappiness, that had grown since she had discovered about Adam and Selina.

In a way, she seemed to be carrying their guilt, because she should have done something about it. But how could she have told her father that his greatly admired protégé and partner was secretly seeing his wife?

Coming abruptly back to the present, Kirsty got up and switched off the television. The screen had gone blank long ago, the station closed down, and now she felt tired—tired and angry. She had got over all that ages ago and had really made a success of life, in spite of Adam's misgivings. Every time she saw her father, though, she was reminded that three people were living a lie, two of them wilfully and one of them, her father, being deceived daily. There was nothing she could do without causing a good deal of hurt to the only person she really cared about.

Her father rang in the morning before she had even opened the gallery. Kirsty had been half expecting it, because if Selina wanted something she simply went on and on until she got it.

'Kirsty, could you find it in your heart to come back home for a while?' he asked straight away, and Kirsty's lips twisted wryly. There it was, victory to Selina, because when she heard the way his voice sounded—so weary—Kirsty knew she could not refuse.

'Selina rang,' she admitted. 'I understand she's off to Paris?'

'One of those endless buying trips,' her father told her. 'I wouldn't trouble you, but I do have a few people coming next week and it's too late to put them off.'

It did occur to Kirsty to ask if Selina had given any thought to the visitors, but she just could not bother. In a way, it would be good to be back home for a while, to see the old places, maybe look up a few old friends and enjoy the house and grounds without the threat of either Selina or Adam around. She nibbled at her lip as it occurred to her that Adam Frazer might very well be among the people coming. Her father often had business meetings at home, and if it was a business meeting then she could hardly expect the mighty Adam Frazer to be left out.

'I can't cater for hordes,' she reminded him, and he laughed, evidently sensing that she would come.

'No catering required,' he assured her. 'I just need a hostess. The usual people will do the catering and then, of course, there's Mrs Drew.'

Yes, there was Mrs Drew! Kirsty frowned as she thought of the sour-faced woman who ostensibly ran Parbury Hall. When her mother had been alive, a couple of dailies from the village had sufficed, but of course Selina had needed a housekeeper, and she had picked one out for herself as soon as she had been established there.

Mrs Drew was the answer to her prayers, she had said, but the woman had been an added nightmare to Kirsty, one she had gladly escaped from when she went to school. The housekeeper had quickly picked up the atmosphere, and she too had learned to skirt round the master of the house and play up to the mistress. Kirsty had been looked at with scornful eyes and ignored.

If anything, the thought of that woman made Kirsty more ready to oblige her father now. It would be interesting to see how Mrs Drew felt about a twenty-four-year-old woman in the house, who had got her summed up.

'When do you want me to come?' she asked without more ado, and she actually heard her father's sigh of relief.

'This second,' he laughed. 'But I expect you have to sort things out at that end?'

'You could say that,' Kirsty replied ruefully. There was a sale coming up the day after tomorrow and she had already been to the viewing. There was another setter there *and* a husky. She brightened as she remembered exactly where it was—about ten miles from her home village.

'I'll be there tomorrow afternoon,' she said eagerly. 'There's a sale about ten miles away from the hall and I can attend it the next day. It fits in fairly well, and I'm sure I can get Susan to work longer while I'm away.'

'See you tomorrow, then,' her father said gleefully. 'You've got this gallery business sorted right down to the fine details, haven't you, darling? You astonish me.'

Kirsty laughed and rang off. She astonished herself, because she had not asked about the visitors. She had allowed her mind to sidetrack to the odious Mrs Drew. Old skeletons! But she didn't know who was coming, and it was possible that Adam would be there.

Her face froze. What was she thinking of? Adam would be in Paris with Selina. She glanced at herself in the nearby mirror, her disgust staring back at her. She only had to think of him and the last time she had seen him came clearly to her memory. It was a good thing to be going back, after all. It was time a few cobwebs were dusted out of her mind, and it was also time that a few skeletons were shaken. She smiled at the thought of shaking the acid-featured Mrs Drew. She wondered how that lady would take it when she was given a few orders by the 'child'.

Kirsty went down to open the gallery, preparing herself to coax Susan into extra work. It was only then that she realised she hadn't asked her father how long she would be required as a hostess. Still, she would play it as it came, and if necessary make a trip down to London to coax Susan further.

CHAPTER TWO

As she drove in between the huge stone pillars that marked the entrance to the grounds of Parbury Hall, Kirsty felt a stirring of the old feelings she had had here long ago, when her mother had been alive and every day had been joyous.

She glanced upwards and smiled. When she had been very young, she had wanted her father to replace the huge stone balls that topped the pillars. She had wanted two griffins. Now she knew that the stone pillars were an exact match with the front of the house; the stone balustrades that led from the huge front windows and went down the steps to the sloping lawns were similarly topped.

There was almost a dread inside her, a fear that something would have changed, because this place had meant so much to her when she was a child and while she had been away it had remained in her head, like a picture of perfection.

There were curtains up at the windows of the lodge that stood at the gate and this disconcerted her for a moment. Nobody had lived there for ages, and although it was scrupulously maintained, along with the hall, it was unoccupied—unless her father had thrown Mrs Drew out and made her stay there. Kirsty smiled at the idea. No such luck. Maybe the lodge was being let to someone from the village, although this surprised her. Surely Selina would not have allowed it? She would know soon enough, anyway, and Kirsty drove on, up the long, twisting drive, waiting for her first glimpse of Parbury Hall.

It appeared as she rounded the last bend in the drive, a lovely old house that stood against a backdrop of high trees. At the moment the lawns were banked by azaleas in full bloom, the sunlight picking up the brilliant colours, and her shoulders relaxed. Nothing had changed. It was almost a fairytale picture.

As she stopped in front of the hall her father came out to meet her instantly, his face wreathed in smiles and his arms wide to welcome her.

'Kirsty! You don't know how good it is to have you back home!' He clasped her close, and Kirsty hid her tear-filled eyes against his shoulder. It was good to be back home, but it would be for a very short time and even that was merely because Selina was away.

Selina had never meant her to be here, and how well she had succeeded with her plans. Anger mixed with sadness and burned for a second in Kirsty, stiffening her, making the tears vanish. She was not a child now, and this would not do at all. What was past was past, and no amount of grieving could alter anything. Grief had never brought her mother back, and grief would not return things to the happy past, to the days before Selina, when Adam had been her hero and shielded her from everything.

'Come inside,' her father said gruffly. 'I won't be absolutely sure that you're back until I see you under this roof.' They both laughed, but Kirsty knew what he meant. It was no longer her right. That had been taken away a long time ago.

As they walked into the vast hallway Mrs Drew appeared, and by this time Kirsty was in exactly the mood

to face her. The sight of the woman brought too many
bad memories.

'Good afternoon, Miss Sinclair.' The face had not im-
proved, Kirsty noted. A frosty old boot came to mind,
and she gave a very frosty smile of her own.

'Good afternoon,' she said briefly. 'My luggage is in
the car, if you would take it up. I trust you have my old
room ready for me?'

Kirsty turned away, winding her arm into her father's
and heading for the small sitting-room where the
afternoon sun turned the place to gold. She had the satisfaction of seeing the acid face turn red with annoyance
and the extra satisfaction of feeling her father's laughter,
right down her arm.

'Beginning as you mean to go on?' he asked with a
wide grin, as the door closed behind them.

'Well, she *is* the housekeeper,' Kirsty mused. 'The
perfect person if you're given to Victorian melodrama.
We wouldn't want her to be overcome by mirth, would
we?'

'We wouldn't get the chance,' her father laughed. 'I'm
expecting her in here any moment to give notice.'

'If she does, then I'll be only too happy to take her
place temporarily,' Kirsty said, flinging herself down on
the settee and smiling up at him.

'A bit of your own back, darling?'

'Just beginning as I mean to go on, as you said,' Kirsty
murmured, adding, 'By the way, I noticed curtains up
at the windows of the lodge. Have you let it out to
someone?'

'Not exactly.' Her father brought a tray of tea across
to her, which had obviously been efficiently served as
soon as her car had stopped in front of the hall. 'Serve,
will you?' he asked, and as she looked up at him ques-

tioningly he finished, 'Adam is living at the lodge for the time being. A couple of weeks, I would think. His own place is being redecorated. He moved in at the lodge last week. He'll be here for dinner tonight. He dines with me in the evening, no sense in doing otherwise, and I enjoy his company.'

Kirsty just stared at him, her brain temporarily numbed. For a few crazy minutes she couldn't even think straight, and it was only her stunned feelings that prevented her from blurting out the words that seemed to be burned across her mind. But why isn't he in Paris with Selina?

It was only as she regained control of herself that she realised how very close she had come to actually saying the words, and she came back to the present to find that her father had apparently noticed nothing at all. She busied herself pouring tea, thankful that he seemed to expect no comment about his bombshell.

Why should he, after all? She was the one who had always been away. Adam had never changed his habits. He had been coming here for years, so why should she have imagined that anything had changed at all?

In any case, it was a good excuse to be close to Selina when he was in this house, and her father's trusting ways would never allow for any suspicion, no matter how often they were together. In the past he had taken one look at the way she herself had got on so well with Adam and left the matter alone. He was such an astute businessman, but he seemed to be utterly incapable of judging those close to him.

It was going to be difficult, more difficult than she could ever have envisaged. She could not face Adam with any show of friendliness, or even with any sort of normality. The last time she had seen him was still too firmly set in her mind, even though it was four years ago. Nothing would erase that and Adam must be well aware of it.

Panic threatened to take hold of her, and she had to fight it down. She had thought herself safe here for a while but she had been wrong. It would have been better to find Selina here. She could fight Selina openly, but Adam was much too subtle for open conflict, and he was so close to her father too.

Later, up in her room, Kirsty stared out of the window across the sweep of lawn, with its banks of glowing azaleas, and down to the lodge. It was not possible actually to see it from here. The gates and the lodge that guarded them were not close to the house. The long, winding drive with tall beech trees hid everything from view, but in her mind she could see it, and she could also see the man who would be there soon, even if he was not there now.

This impossible situation had been sprung on her without warning and she was not exactly sure if she could face it. There would be just the three of them for dinner and nobody at all to help with conversation. She could just imagine Adam's sardonic face as he met her, and even now she felt those cold grey eyes boring into her.

She turned away from the window impatiently. She would have to face him because there was no way out of it. Why wasn't he with Selina? They would have worked out some plan, of course. Maybe he was going to join her later. Selina had not actually said how long she would be away, and her father had not mentioned his wife at all, but she would have worked out something to enable her to meet Adam.

It was only as she turned back to her room that Kirsty noticed that the décor was still the same: white walls, softly flowered covers on the bed, and matching curtains. It had been redecorated over the years but essentially it was still the same, and she knew that this could be placed with her father. Left to herself, Selina would probably have had the room stripped out and made into a store-room.

Her cases were there, as ordered, and she smiled grimly to herself. This internal panic was childish. She was much older now than when she had last seen Adam, and it was only the tinglings of the past that made her feel like this. She unpacked and sorted her things into the drawers and wardrobe, trying to keep her mind blank.

A long, warm bath would probably do the trick, and she was pleased to find that her bathroom was exactly the same too. She ran the bath and stepped into it, sinking into the water and allowing it to soothe away both the journey here and the shock of discovering that Adam would be facing her very soon.

He was so deeply rooted in her life that she could hardly think of her own home without him there. She snorted with annoyance and sank more deeply into the warm, scented water. It was ridiculous! She was a success, running a thriving business and her own life with no problems at all. Here in this house, though, the past clung insidiously, both the happy past and the past that held Selina.

The beautiful face, the blonde hair and blue eyes, came into her mind as if her stepmother was right there at that moment. Nothing ever went wrong for Selina, and though Kirsty could congratulate herself about her small and thriving business, Selina had made quite a success too, because she had launched into the fashion world, clothes always having been dear to her heart.

While Kirsty had still been at school, Selina had coaxed her husband into backing her in a boutique, and with his money and her skill it had been a winner. Now she had several boutiques, and for the launch of the last one, four years ago, Kirsty had been foolish enough to allow her father to persuade her to attend. That evening had finally put the last brick into the wall she had built against Adam Frazer.

It had to be admitted that Selina knew how to launch a venture. The affair had been quite a glittering occasion and, forewarned by her father, Kirsty had been glittering too. She had been just twenty, and it was the last time she had seen Adam.

Somehow, she had not really expected him to be there. Even so, she had felt the need for security, even if only against Selina, and she had invited Karen Swift, who was still a friend.

'You look stunning!' Karen had arrived at Kirsty's flat early so that they could share a taxi, and she had walked round Kirsty with admiring eyes. 'Red is your colour.' She had grimaced wryly. 'Correction, *any* colour is your colour.'

It was perfectly true. With nut-brown hair that swung to her shoulders in gentle waves and wide green eyes, Kirsty could wear almost any colour at all, but tonight she had chosen a red dress in silk, a very expensive present from her father for her birthday the week before. It was when he had taken her out for a birthday meal that he had beguiled her into attending this function that she now very much dreaded. The glamorous dress was her only shield.

'Gosh! It's like a first night,' Karen muttered as their taxi dropped them off in the West End. 'People arriving in bus-loads!'

Not exactly, Kirsty mused, but the impression was there, and once inside the feeling of being surrounded with one's superiors simply grew. That was coming from Selina, of course. Ostensibly, these were people invited to have a preview of the clothes, but as far as Kirsty could see there was not much previewing going on; it was just an expensive party.

Presumably, all the other boutiques had been launched like this, but Kirsty had never been to any of those. She glanced at her watch and wondered how soon she could make a dignified retreat, but she knew she would have to stay for at least some of the time. Her father was there and homed in on her immediately, and, as Karen was simply drooling over the whole affair, Kirsty was stuck.

Selina gave her a cold look and then ignored her, and Kirsty wondered what her father thought of it. She felt as left out of things as she had always done. Extra years had not changed that.

She managed very well, even so, until she looked up a little later and saw Adam in deep conversation with Selina. The sight of him, of both of them together, brought the past rushing back with a bitterness that quite shocked her. Nothing had changed. She shouldn't be here. She was outside all this and outside their lives. She turned and made for the door, looking round rather frantically for Karen but only encountering her father again.

'Darling, where are you off to?' he asked worriedly. 'You've gone quite pale.'

'I've got a headache,' she managed, hating herself for lying. It seemed to her that she had been lying by omission for a very long time, and now a downright lie simply made her more miserable. 'I—I was looking for

Karen. When I get a headache, I just have to go. You know that.'

He did. She had often had minor attacks of migraine when she was younger and her father had no idea that they had stopped, probably because she was not in any way connected with Selina now. It was an excuse that had sprung straight to her mind, and she felt ashamed that he believed her.

'I'll find Karen for you,' he assured her quickly. 'You stay there, love, and I'll get her.'

At least it meant that she would not be at loggerheads with her father about rushing off, and Kirsty leaned against the wall, deliberately keeping her eyes down. Just a little while and she would be out of this. She didn't know any of these people, she didn't want to know them, and she couldn't bear seeing Adam.

Her father was just returning with Karen in tow when Adam came up, his face alert as he saw Kirsty.

'Going so soon?' The faintly ironic voice had Kirsty's head coming up quickly, and his eyes captured hers and held them with ease. He thought she was running out and she was not about to enlighten him. The shock of seeing him was more than she could cope with.

He had changed, hardened, the planes of his face now more austere. There was no softness in him. The grey eyes were more defined than she remembered. They glittered, mocked, pinned her fast with no sympathy at all. She had imagined, this last year, that she was settled into womanhood, but, facing Adam, she felt like a girl again. He looked ruthless beyond belief, magnificent and remote.

'She's got one of her migraines coming, by the look of it.' Her father explained for her when she was not able to utter a word herself, and Kirsty pulled herself out of the feeling of anxious awe that Adam's unexpected presence had forced her into. This was nothing to do with him, and in a moment she would be away from here.

'I'll get a taxi,' she managed quickly. 'Sorry about this, Karen.'

'Don't mind me. It's been an experience,' Karen assured her with a grin. 'Too much of this stuff would go to my head, anyhow.'

Unfortunately it was pouring with rain as Kirsty pulled the door open, and in any case Donald Sinclair was clearly worried by Kirsty's pale face.

'Forget the taxi,' he ordered gruffly. 'I'll take you both home.'

'Oh, darling!' Selina came up and wound her arm into her husband's. 'I can't cope if you desert me.' It was clear that she had no intention of being upstaged, and before anything could be said, Adam volunteered.

'Don't worry, Donald. I'll take them home. You stay here and keep an eye on your wife.'

'You think I need looking after, Adam?' Selina gurgled seductively, and Kirsty's lips tightened before she could stop them. Much more of this and the headache would be all too real.

'We'll get a taxi,' she insisted stiffly, but Adam took her arm, ignoring Selina's words and opening the door again.

'I'll take you,' he announced harshly. 'Wait here, I'm parked just a few yards away.'

And Kirsty found herself under the awning of the boutique, the rain lashing down a few inches away as Adam went for his car. She had been whirled into the situation almost before she could think, and once again she was at the mercy of Adam and, in a way, Selina.

'Come inside, darling,' Selina urged, gripping her husband's arm. 'Kirsty isn't a child. She proved that when she went off by herself. She doesn't need you, but I do.'

'I'll ring you later,' Donald Sinclair said distractedly as he was pulled back inside, and Kirsty felt only relief as the door swung shut. He would ring her, she knew, but she also knew that the hold Selina had on him would not allow more than a few seconds' conversation. She would rather have had a taxi too. In fact, she would rather have been soaking wet than travel with Adam.

'Adam Frazer is a very forceful man,' Karen mused, drawing further back into the doorway, and Kirsty wasn't quite sure what she meant, although she could have been comparing Adam's unwarranted intervention with her father's uneasy withdrawal from the scene.

She wasn't bothered. All she wanted was to get out of there, and if she had to put up with Adam *en route* then so be it. She would have no need to speak because he looked as if he would not even glance at her. At least she was not alone with him. She had Karen there.

She did not have Karen there.

'I'll drop you off first,' Adam announced, glancing briefly at Karen as he pulled away from the kerb after picking them up. He must have dived between the raindrops because he didn't seem to be wet at all, although his car had been out of sight. It was a new Mercedes and Kirsty was glad of the warmth and comfort.

She had managed to get herself wet just going from the awning to the car and Adam had almost thrown her into the passenger seat, giving her no choice at all. Karen was in the back, and that was exactly where Kirsty had intended to be herself.

'Don't bother,' Karen said breezily. 'I'll get a taxi from Kirsty's flat. I live a good way off, right out of your way.'

'No trouble,' Adam stated flatly. 'It's raining hard and you may have trouble getting a taxi. It's simple enough to get you home, just tell me where.'

That settled everything, and Kirsty could almost hear Karen's quizzical expression from the back of the car. He certainly was a forceful character. She had never noticed before, although it was true that he always seemed to get his own way without raising his voice. He had never been hard, as he was now, though.

She shivered and Adam glanced at her.

'Cold?' She had never noticed before how dark his voice was either, and now it worried her even more. Instinct told her she should not be here.

'Not really. I got a little wet.' The words seemed to come out shakily, and Adam glanced at her again, but he said nothing. Kirsty felt that she was holding herself together with great difficulty. There was a terrible atmosphere of waiting, and she wondered if Karen felt it too.

When they finally got to Karen's house Kirsty was still shivering, and as they dropped Karen off Adam shrugged out of his jacket and placed it around Kirsty's shoulders.

'I don't want——' she began, but he enclosed her in the warmth all the same.

'You don't want to be surrounded by anything that's me?' he enquired cynically. 'Just look upon it as an inanimate object that might protect you from pneumonia. Forget I ever saw it.'

Kirsty said nothing at all. She was unlikely to forget he had ever seen it. She could feel the warmth from his body and smell the faint tang of aftershave that clung to the jacket. It was a scent she remembered from the past and, far from feeling surrounded by an inanimate object, she felt surrounded by Adam. She bit into her lower lip anxiously. At this rate the headache would be real, and she would be begging for a tablet long before they got back.

She did not, however, because Adam didn't speak again, and it was only as they reached her flat that problems arose. The rain was worse, by now pouring down, and Adam took one look at it, reached into the side-pocket of the car and brought out an umbrella.

'Be prepared,' he muttered wryly as she looked at him in astonishment. 'I'm not the sort to roam around with a furled umbrella, but this one is nicely chunky and opens out to a good size. Wait there.'

Before she could protest he was out of the car with the umbrella up, and making his way determinedly to her side.

'Your jacket,' she managed feebly, but he took her arm and urged her to the steps.

'When we get inside,' he assured her smoothly, and that was when Kirsty stiffened. He was not coming inside.

'Have it now and lend me your umbrella,' she insisted, but he stood and eyed her sardonically.

'No way. I'd rather lend you the jacket. I have plenty of jackets but only one umbrella. I'm keeping it. Come along.'

Kirsty could hardly make a scene, and the fact that the door of the flat opened directly into the road made exchanging the objects impossible without both of them getting wet. She had the uneasy feeling that he had thought of that, but there was no way of getting out of it.

There was something about him that worried her. He was not in any way the same. He was not Adam as she remembered him, and once in the flat she took off the jacket speedily, looking at him as if she expected him to leave at once.

'Coffee?' he asked with taunting amusement, and once again he had her at a decided disadvantage. He had left the party to bring her home, taken Karen all that way, and saved her from a soaking. It seemed quite uncivil to tell him to go now, and in any case she didn't have the courage. He was a cold stranger.

'I'll put the kettle on,' she muttered, trying to avoid his eyes and still appear normal. 'I've only got instant.'

'Suits me,' he assured her, adding quietly, 'You should get out of that beautiful dress before you catch your death of cold.'

'I'm warm now,' Kirsty stated. She was, because she could still feel the heat from his jacket. It had been quite alarming, the loss she had felt as she had taken it off to give it back.

'You'd be warmer in a nice thick dressing-gown,' he suggested darkly, and her cheeks flushed even more. What was wrong with her? He was an old friend who was now an enemy. What did she care what he said? She looked up defiantly and was caught by the cool grey gaze.

Until then she had merely been listening to his voice, worried about it, but now she saw the way his eyes were moving over her, making a detailed inspection of her face, lingering on the way the dress clung to her breasts.

'I'll make the coffee,' she managed in a brittle, flustered voice, and disappeared into the small kitchen, her heart pounding like a drum. Her heart had pounded when she was seventeen, that summer when her world had shattered. He had looked at her then, but not as he was looking now. Now it was a cold-blooded assessment, frightening.

As she was making the coffee she could hear him wandering about the flat, and she didn't know whether to rush in with the drink and get rid of him fast or hide here and hope he would tire of waiting and go. There was no chance of the latter. He appeared at the kitchen door and draped himself against the jamb, watching her.

'You've made the place nice,' he offered, and Kirsty found her cheeks flushing again, this time with remembered annoyance, and her anxiety momentarily deserted her.

'You expected I would continue to live in squalor?'

'Ouch!' he said softly. 'Forget I ever said that. I was angry and frustrated.'

'I fail to see why you should be angry and frustrated about *my* life,' Kirsty countered, and he took his coffee deftly from her hand, walking back into the other room with it.

'Can't you?' he asked quietly. 'I was afraid you would come to no good. You were my little angel, gone very sadly astray.'

'I was never an angel,' Kirsty said hotly, incensed that he was making her feel even more inferior, and he turned slowly to look at her.

'That's how I thought of you once, a long time ago.' He stared at her steadily for a few unnerving seconds and then turned away again. 'I hear you gave up the art school course.'

It was an unexpected attack and Kirsty couldn't answer for a second. Truth to tell, she had been too unhappy to settle to anything, and for the past few months she had been living on the money her mother had left her.

Now, though, she had an idea, and she had been working on it for quite a while. Her own art gallery.

It would be a peaceful place to hide herself. She had spent lots of time at auctions as she had furnished her flat and she found it stimulating, and all the good pictures she had on the walls had been picked up for very little. She had already discussed her ideas with her father and she hoped frantically that he had not told Adam.

'Yes,' she answered at last. She considered leaving it at that but he was staring at her again in that disconcerting way, and she felt compelled to offer further explanations. 'As it happened, I *did* have talent, in spite of your misgivings, but I decided to give it up.'

'Why?' The grey eyes were still on her and Kirsty moved impatiently.

'I suppose I wasn't happy.' She told herself that if he asked why once again she would scream at him, but he did no such thing. To her vast annoyance he simply sat down to drink his coffee, looking as if he had every intention of staying for a while, his eyes still summing her up.

'Don't you have something to do?' Kirsty questioned waspishly.

'Such as what?' Evidently he had decided to play this cat-and-mouse game, but Kirsty was not about to join in.

'Such as getting back to the opening of the boutique. You're missing all the glitter.'

'You're glittering quite enough for me,' he murmured, his eyes moving over her again. 'What happened to the headache?'

Kirsty felt her cheeks begin to burn. Once more, it was an unexpected attack. She had quite forgotten about her excuse, but it was clear that Adam had forgotten nothing.

'It seems to have gone off.'

'Then, let's go back together,' he suggested smoothly, and Kirsty glared at him.

'Thank you, but no. I can do without that kind of company.'

'Mine or Selina's?' He was now watching her with narrowed eyes; everything about him was telling her to beware. Unfortunately, Kirsty was in no mood to beware. He had wound her up, and as far as she could see he had done it deliberately.

'Both,' she said coldly. 'There's little to choose between you.'

He got slowly to his feet, his coffee discarded, and the look on his face should have warned her to keep silent. She could see intense power and she had already seen the coldness.

'You're twenty now, Kirsty,' he reminded her. 'Quite old enough to be responsible for your own words. I want an explanation of those particular words.'

'Oh, stop pretending!' Kirsty flung away and then turned back furiously, the hurt and anger flooding to the surface as if it had never been away. 'You can pretend with my father, but don't try it with me. In any case, I would imagine that almost everyone else knows, it's been going on long enough. Anybody only has to see the two of you together to know!'

'Be very explicit.' There was a quiet menace in his voice but it failed to register in Kirsty's mind. She was too stunned at the way this was hurting, even after three years. He wasn't even the same, but the feeling of loss was there, as if no time had passed at all, and she wanted to strike out, to hurt back.

'You're having an affair with my father's wife! Is that explicit enough for you?' she raged. 'And don't bother to deny it. I *heard* you! I heard both of you the night that my father made you a partner.' He took a step towards her, but she was in full swing and gave no thought to caution. 'I wasn't the only one who heard you, either,' she continued hotly. 'Karen was in the next room to me and she heard you—billing and cooing!'

She felt childish as soon as she had said those particular words, because they were words out of the past and now she was no longer a girl, but they had stuck in her mind, painting erotic pictures that threatened to choke her, and now they were out before she could stop them.

Adam pounced on her before she could even give any thought to danger, and she found herself looking up into a face so furious and alien that she felt afraid.

'You believe that of me?' he asked harshly. 'You've thought that for three years?'

'I've *known* it for three years! I believe the evidence of my own ears, and why not, after all? You have it all your way now, don't you? You have equal status with my father, you practically run the place, and he's told me over and over that if you went away he wouldn't know where to turn on the financial front. You've got him just where you want him, and you've got his wife.' She struggled in his grasp. 'Why don't you announce it and let the rest of us be rid of her?'

'Why haven't you announced it?' His face was very close, white with rage, and his fingers were biting into her skin, but Kirsty was too angry to feel endangered.

'It would kill Daddy, and you know it,' she bit out through clenched teeth. 'You were a stranger who came into our lives and you've gained control of everything. I hate you, Adam Frazer, and one day I'll pay you back.'

For a second she thought he was going to strike her. He seemed to freeze, his expression icing over, the grey eyes narrowing, but instead of the violence she had expected he moved closer, forcing her back against the closed door, trapping her there with his body. His thighs were pressed against hers and she could feel the heat of his skin through the thin silk of his white shirt.

Strange feelings raced through her and she panicked, beating her closed fists against his chest.

'Let me go!' She was so scared of her own reactions that her head was banging against the hard wood of the door, and he curved his hand round her nape, jerking her head forward, tilting it to his.

'You threatened to pay me back. Pay me back now, Kirsty,' he suggested in a menacing voice. 'Pay me back for all the years of affection I gave you and then we'll call it quits, because you were not worth one minute of my time, after all.'

CHAPTER THREE

KIRSTY had no chance even to think about what he meant, because before she could struggle his mouth covered hers for the first time ever, and there was such ferocity about it that Kirsty went cold all over.

She clenched her teeth, tightened her lips, attempted to twist her head away, fighting in any way she could, but she was no match for the strength of a powerful, determined man. He subdued her almost contemptuously, his hand gripping her chin, never letting the contact of their lips break for a second as he forced himself closer.

He was making her frighteningly aware of the muscled power of the body that pressed her against the door, too aware of the warm, tangy smell of his skin. She felt herself weakening and she opened panic-stricken eyes, but his own eyes were also open, too close to her, the cold grey burning into her, and she shut her eyes fast.

Having her trapped so securely he had no need to restrain her further, and his free hand ran slowly down her spine, tracing every small bone, until she was arched against him with no escape possible, a melting sensation growing inside that had her murmuring in fright.

He moved slowly against her, his hands holding her close, and her body gave in, became fluid, the tension dying away, and even his low growl of satisfaction did nothing to bring her to her senses. His lips softened and circled hers determinedly until, with a small cry of shame, her mouth opened to the fiery invasion of his tongue.

It was the first time she had felt such a thing and everything inside her seemed to explode with longing. The excitement was unbearable, and she did not even consider anything but her own desire. She pressed against him eagerly as fire flooded her veins, and he ran his hands down her thighs, holding her against him with sure expertise. There was such an intensity of feeling that she had no idea how she was behaving, and he was fuelling her desire, slowly and deliberately.

Her hands sought his neck, her fingers tugging at the thick, silky texture of his hair and her mind vaguely wondering why she had never noticed before how beautiful it was. Her other hand moved against the hard curve of his jawline, and she was only dimly aware that she was kissing him back with an abandoned hunger that he was encouraging with every movement of his hard body.

She was too dazed to react immediately when Adam jerked his head away and stared down into her bewildered face, and it was a few seconds before she realised that he was watching her with cool indifference. He looked down at her with an aloof detachment that brought colour flooding into her face, and it was only then that Kirsty understood how thoroughly he had humiliated her.

'I loathe you! You're disgusting!' She could hear how shaken her voice sounded, but not one ounce of pity showed on his coldly handsome face.

'Probably,' he surmised unfeelingly. 'Still, for a while there you were very anxious to take your stepmother's place in my bed, weren't you?'

He moved back, freeing her, and Kirsty hit him with her flat hand, all her humiliation and frustration behind the action. He didn't even attempt to evade the blow, and for a second he smiled at her callously, his eyes narrowed and watchful.

'Was that disgust with me or disgust with yourself?' he asked drily. He turned to the door, his glance skimming over her disparagingly, noting the way her chest rose and fell with suppressed emotion. She could feel the hectic spots of colour in her cheeks and she clenched her hands as his eyes rested on the swollen fullness of her breasts.

'Very nice,' he drawled sardonically. 'But you're not exactly an angel, are you, Kirsty?'

He went out, closing the door quietly, and Kirsty just sank to the floor on the spot. She had been given a lesson in sexual arousal and she was shocked and repelled by her own actions. She had shown no control at all. The moment that fear of his anger had left her mind she had been ardently begging for more, trying to erase an empty feeling inside that had come from nowhere. He had robbed her of her sanity and her self-esteem, and the thought of ever seeing him again made her shudder.

Well, she would be seeing him tonight. Kirsty shook herself from the past and moved to get out of the bath. She had been lying there thinking for a long time, and the water was getting cold. She would face Adam and never flinch. He had not come out of that last encounter with any honour, and all the guilt should be his.

It had been four years ago. She was completely grown-up now. Emotion did not send her reeling. She had Guy, and never sank into that blazing world Adam had forced on her then. She was always in control. Her encounter with Adam had been the result of many things, but mostly it had been immaturity.

She dried herself and regarded her image in the mirror dispassionately. She was tall, almost exactly the same height as Guy, which was comforting, unthreatening. She was still as slender as she had been four years ago with the same high, tilted breasts and long legs. Her hair, damp from the steaming water, curled around her shoulders, a glowing brown that shone in the light, and the long green eyes looked back at her fearlessly.

Kirsty was annoyed and it showed on her face. Her annoyance was with herself, that she should have spent so long mulling over the past. For a little while she was her father's hostess, and it was time she assumed that role. Glancing at her watch, she noticed that it was already six-thirty, and not for any reason at all would she arrive down those stairs in a last-minute panic.

She dressed carefully, selecting a chiffon dress in multi-colours of brown and orange on a cream background. It drifted around her, complementing her hair colour and bringing out the clear green of her eyes. She stood back and regarded herself with satisfaction. Looking like this, she could face anyone. She now had the sophistication she had lacked four years ago, and Adam was not going to disconcert her.

Her father was in the drawing-room when she went down, and as she opened the door the first thing her eyes fell on was the portrait of her mother that hung, as it always had, over the huge fireplace. It didn't hurt now to look at it, and Kirsty stood silently, just looking up at the lovely face.

'She was beautiful.' She murmured the words as her father came to stand beside her.

'She was,' he agreed quietly. 'But I wouldn't go around saying that, if I were you. You're exactly like her. Some people would think you were boasting.' There was humour in his voice and Kirsty was glad to hear it. It meant that he too could stand and look at the portrait of her mother without the aching grief that had been there for so long.

'Why——?' she began, and then stopped abruptly. She had been about to ask why he kept it there. It was a great surprise, because she would have thought that Selina would object.

'Why is it still there? It has always been there. It belongs there.' Kirsty glanced at him when she heard the almost harsh determination in his voice. There was something here she wasn't quite picking up, but he smiled at her and moved away. 'A drink before dinner?'

Kirsty nodded, but as she turned to follow him across the room she stopped, her whole body stiffening in shock. Adam was standing silently in the doorway, watching her, and she had no idea how long he had been there. He was observing her dispassionately, as if she were some object behind a plate-glass window, and it was only as her father noticed him too that any expression at all came to his face.

It seemed to her that the last four years had hardened him even further. Oh, she recognised him, but there the likeness ended. He was a cynical stranger as far as she could see, with nothing in his face that could remind her of the man she had known for so long.

'The prodigal daughter,' he remarked drily and Kirsty knew she would have problems with him while she was here. Even with her father there, Adam could not pretend. He had not forgotten their encounter four years ago, and the grey eyes were icy as the waters of a frozen lake.

'She's taking Selina's role on board for a while,' Donald Sinclair said happily, his arm coming round Kirsty's shoulders, and Adam detached himself from the doorway and walked slowly into the room.

'Is she capable?' he enquired lazily, and Kirsty tried not to stiffen, glad when her father took it as a joke. Thinking of him upstairs, such a short time ago, had left her a little vulnerable, and she no longer felt quite so cool and sure of herself.

'She's grown-up now, Adam,' her father pointed out. 'You'll have to change your way of dealing with her. She's no longer your little pet.'

'Obviously,' Adam murmured, his eyes still on Kirsty's face. 'Don't worry, I'll treat her very differently.' He glanced up at the portrait they had both been admiring. 'A remarkable likeness. How about the character?'

'Kirsty is more spirited——' Donald began, and Adam interrupted sardonically.

'You're excusing her bad temper before it becomes evident?'

'She's sparky,' her father laughed.

'And present at this moment,' Kirsty finished angrily, her eyes beginning to give off sparks of their own. She held out her hand, her momentary shock at seeing him under control. 'Good evening, Adam. How are you?'

'Humbled by the sight of you,' he assured her with a cool smile. 'I'm sorry that your duties here will be hampered by my stay at the lodge. Still, I'll only be one more person to deal with, and you're quite used to dealing with me, after all.'

Kirsty was still staring into his cold eyes as Mrs Drew came to the door and announced that the meal was ready.

'I'm about to serve dinner, sir,' she stated, ignoring Kirsty, and Kirsty reacted immediately.

'Thank you. We'll be there when we've had our drinks. We're not quite ready yet.'

Adam's eyes narrowed, slight surprise at the back of the cold grey, and Donald Sinclair's lips twisted in amusement.

'Round two, Kirsty,' he said in a low voice. 'Keep going. With a bit of luck we'll be rid of her before Selina comes back.'

Kirsty smiled grimly. Not much chance of that, and even if it came to pass, Selina would immediately seek the woman out and reinstate her. In any case, if Adam was going to be here frequently, she would make her own stay here as short as possible. She had not missed the icy anger at the back of his voice, and the way he had walked slowly into the room had made her shiver. There had been a look of the stalking animal about him.

Standing next to him, as her father poured the drinks, she was very much aware of his lean height. Not long ago she had been thinking of Guy and his height, considering how comforting it was that he did not tower over her. Adam towered over her. Of course he always had, but she had never noticed it as she was noticing it now.

There was something about Adam that made her feel helpless, almost fragile, and she could only think that it was his physique. It might, of course, have been something to do with his brainpower. There was plenty of that. Perhaps that was the reason for the feeling that was almost singing through the air, because she knew he was as irritatingly aware of her as she was of him.

He turned and looked down at her, observing her green-eyed scrutiny.

'Almost like old times,' he said sardonically, as her father moved away briefly to answer the telephone.

'Not at all like old times,' Kirsty replied shortly. 'I look at the world through different eyes now.'

His glance skimmed over her face, and then she saw the rather cruel smile she had noticed before on several occasions.

'I'm sure you'll bear it for the necessary time. Then you can scuttle back to your little shop.' The derision stung her into anger and her eyes flashed at him furiously, the irritation that she could not speak her mind with her father close and about to return at any moment showing on her face.

'It's a gallery!' she snapped in a low voice. 'I am now very well-known!'

'Really? I must come along and browse. I need new pictures for my place.'

'I specialise in animals,' Kirsty fumed, and his dark brows rose in mocking surprise as he watched her closely.

'Now, why would you think I didn't know that? Donald and I spend hours discussing you. As to animals, I would have thought that very appropriate for me. You seem to rate me at jungle level.'

'I don't rate you at all!' Kirsty snapped. 'And I don't do snakes!'

He laughed, and she could see her mistake. He was enjoying this. He intended to goad her. It would have been better to engage in polite chatter. He might have behaved differently if she had answered more urbanely when he had spoken of old times. It was too late now. The tone was set for the whole of her stay here and she had brought it on herself.

'One of the larger predators, then?' he suggested as her father came back. 'We're discussing Kirsty's gallery,' Adam disclosed. 'I've just given her a commission. She's going to find me a large cat.'

'A cat?' Donald looked startled. 'I didn't realise you had a leaning towards cats.'

'Only the dangerous varieties,' Adam murmured. 'She's going to find me a rapacious hunting creature to fit into my lifestyle and complement my character, aren't you, Kirsty?'

Her father thought it was highly amusing, but Kirsty felt a chill on her skin, because she knew that while she was here Adam would be unlikely to move out of the lodge. He would keep an eye on things and make sure she was not in any mood to warn her father of the secret life his wife led with his most trusted friend.

Next day, Kirsty was up bright and early to make the journey to the sale, and she was just leaving the house when her father called to her from his study.

'Drop in at the lodge as you go past, will you, Kirsty?' he asked. 'I need to speak to Adam and there's no reply. Something seems to be wrong with his phone.'

'Perhaps he's out?' Kirsty offered quickly. She had no desire whatever to call in at the lodge, and even less desire to see Adam. Last night's dinner had been a great strain. The wretched housekeeper had placed her exactly opposite to Adam and every time she'd looked up his eyes had been on her.

It had made her very uncomfortable, especially as she had found herself glancing at him too, when he wasn't looking, and found herself noticing how the light picked up the blue-black shine of his hair. He had looked as perfect as he had ever looked, and it had irritated her beyond words that she noticed.

'He's not out, darling. It's Saturday,' her father reminded her. 'He's not going into the office today and neither am I. We did have a bit of work to do, though, and we're doing it here. I want to remind him to bring the Eastbourne papers. Just call in, there's a good girl.'

Kirsty made a wry face. There's a good girl! Her father still didn't realise that she was grown up. She nodded and set off. Why she should be bothered about stopping at the lodge and facing Adam, she didn't know. All she had to do was sound her horn and shout at him from the car.

When she got to the lodge she did just that, although she didn't get to the shouting bit because Adam didn't acknowledge her signal. The door was open, and although she waited, and sounded the horn several times, he didn't come. She had the feeling he was doing it deliberately, and if he thought she was scared to go to the door he could think again.

Kirsty got out of the car and marched across to the lodge, up the little path, and banged on the partly open front door. She got the same result—nothing. There was no way out of this, she had to go in, and she pushed the door wider and stepped inside.

'Adam!' She called his name loudly and impatiently. She knew he was here somewhere and that this was childish, some stupid game. 'Adam!' Kirsty raised her voice even more, and got much more than she had bargained for. He strolled into the room, towelling his hair, and all that covered him was a white bath-towel tied around his waist.

'You were roaring for me?' he enquired ironically, standing exactly where he was and draping the smaller towel round his neck.

'I blew the horn over and over! I knocked on the door! Why didn't you answer like any civilised person?' She knew it was embarrassment that was sharpening her voice, and it annoyed her even more that he was not one bit embarrassed himself.

'Obviously I was taking a shower,' he explained with taunting patience. 'I don't normally roam about dressed like this, although if I had expected you I might have been tempted to leave the towels in the bathroom.'

'You're disgusting!' Kirsty snapped, her face flushing wildly.

'I know,' he agreed silkily. 'You told me four years ago. I haven't forgotten. So what do you want, Kirsty? Is this a social visit, or have you come to threaten me?'

It was almost laughable to hear those words. He was standing there, six feet two, with a chest like iron and strong arms that could have crushed her. Threaten him! She was the one who felt threatened, because she couldn't seem to get any words out now; she couldn't even take her eyes off the faintly golden skin of his chest and arms.

'Daddy wants you to take some papers up to the hall when you go,' she managed in a choking voice. She clenched her hands and tightened her lips, outraged at her own feelings and his behaviour. 'The Eastbourne papers.'

'Right. Message received.'

When she didn't leave, his eyes ran over her flushed face, and then travelled all the way down her body, lingering on the slender curve of her hips beneath the cream pleated skirt she wore and then moving upwards, to rest on the swell of her breasts beneath the cinnamon-coloured blouse that was neatly tucked in at her waist.

'Is that all?' he asked, when she didn't make any move to go. 'Or is there something I can do for you—personally?'

'Yes! You can drop dead!' Kirsty snapped, turning on her heel and storming out of the lodge. She could hear him laughing even when she got to the car, and she knew that she had walked right into that one with her eyes open.

He had just stood there, and without doing a thing he had been holding her spellbound. No wonder Selina found him essential to her existence. For those few seconds in there he had seemed to be exuding raw sex like a stun-ray. She had almost started to walk towards him. He was disgusting, beastly! Why had she never seen it before?

She drove off, her wheels tossing up stones on the drive, and it was a good while before she calmed down, and only then because she made a vow not to think of him at all. She even said it aloud and the foolishness of that brought her to her senses. She started to laugh, but stopped very quickly when she seemed to hear an echo from Adam. Even his laughter was sensual.

The sale took her mind off him, because she had to fight very hard and keep her nerve to get the husky. It was rather special and beautifully framed, and, with a little quick reckoning up, she decided that it was worth the extra money, even though she would have to charge more than usual. The Irish setter was a bargain, however, and then, just as she was thinking of paying for her treasures and leaving, the auctioneer announced that he would now sell a few late items.

Kirsty stayed, but there was not much to interest her until the very last minute, and then the men brought out a large picture. It was almost twice as big as the others, and when they turned it round for viewing Kirsty leaned forward and felt an odd rush of excitement. It was a panther, and quite one of the best animal studies she had ever seen.

People started to leave quietly and she was stunned to think that nobody else seemed to be interested. Maybe she would not have been interested herself if Adam had not made his sarcastic remarks about giving her a commission to find him one of the big cats. Its size was enough to put people off, and the setting was not normal either. The panther was in a city, its power and ferocity dominating the scene. The streets were deserted, the lights of the buildings shining on a prowling animal whose coat shone like burnished black velvet.

A predator! Kirsty chewed at her lip and then started to bid. Adam thought she was playing at being a success. What a blow to his ego if, the very day after he had mentioned it, she produced an unusual and striking picture that was exactly what he had been talking about.

Of course, if he didn't want it she would be left with it on her hands, but it was worth the risk to get the better of him. In any case, there were only two other people interested, and many had left. She got it for far less than she would have been prepared to pay and the auctioneer positively glared at her as she gave him a cheeky grin.

Driving back to the hall, she felt very pleased with her morning's efforts, and made all sorts of wild plans about how she would confront Adam Frazer in her moment of triumph. By the time she turned in at the gates, however, she was beginning to have second thoughts.

She had the feeling he would laugh, pay an exorbitant price and give it to some charity when she wasn't looking. It would be patronising and would make her feel childish. She wasn't even sure if it hadn't been childish in any case, and when she got out at the hall she left the panther in the car.

Her father was very interested, and came to have a look as she propped the other pictures against the settee in the small sitting-room and knelt down to make a close inspection.

'They're beauties!' her father said enthusiastically. 'Just what my study needs. I'll buy them both.'

'Sorry.' Kirsty looked up at him and laughed, her face glowing with pleasure. 'They're both ordered. The husky is a very special find. You just don't get them, and I've had a customer after one for ages. The setter goes to New York next week. You'll have to let me know what you want. I rarely have anything like this to spare, and I never break collections.'

'Too damned professional,' her father grumbled good-humouredly. 'What do you think, Adam?'

Kirsty looked up with a start of something close to anxiety. She hadn't heard Adam come into the room. She had assumed that he had left already, but he was standing there, looking at her from the door, just like last night. His eyes were running over the way her skirt fell in soft pleats around her as she knelt down, the way her hair brushed her face, and now he looked into the wide green eyes that stared at him with such startled confusion.

Just for one second, Kirsty thought his face looked softened, something of the old Adam about it. There even seemed to be a slight curve to his lips that was not sardonic, but she knew she had been mistaken when he spoke.

'Hard as nails,' he pronounced drily. He came round and looked down at the result of her morning's work. 'What a pity,' he murmured, 'no big cat. I suppose it was asking too much from such a small gallery.'

Kirsty got smoothly to her feet and faced him, although she had to look up a long way to meet the taunting grey eyes.

'Well, I was going to put it on display,' she said briskly, a smile on her lips, although her eyes were flashing dangerously, 'but if you really are so set on a big cat—wait here!'

She marched out of the room before he could make any comment, and inside she was fuming. So this was how he intended to pass his time while she was here with her father. He was going to mock her at every opportunity, and he clearly thought she couldn't find anything if it was difficult. He should come along and see her American and Japanese customers! The only person who sneered at her was Adam Frazer. Not true, she reminded herself, Selina sneered too. How very much alike they were, and how they deserved each other.

She got the panther out of the car and struggled indoors with it, temper giving her extra strength, and when she got back to the sitting-room Adam was laughing with her father. If she had not known her father so well she would have been convinced that they were laughing at her. Adam was getting under her skin, making her feel unsure of herself, and she would have to be much more forceful.

'The cat!' she announced, propping it by the door to give them both a good view. 'One predator, as ordered. It's in beautiful condition, wonderfully framed and in an astonishing setting. I want a thousand for it, on the nose.'

'My God!' Adam came forward, his eyes on the picture, a slow smile of sheer admiration growing across his face. 'You're a miracle, Miss Sinclair. You must have picked that right out of my head.'

'You mean, you actually want it?' Kirsty gasped, staring at him in amazement. She couldn't really believe it. She had only paid five hundred for the panther, and she had asked so much from sheer temper. Adam was the most clever man she had ever met, but he was absolutely enthralled by the picture; she could see that on his face. Her forceful determination drained away.

'Try to back out now and I'll strangle you,' he growled, glancing up at her. 'I know exactly where this is going to go.'

'It—it's too big for an ordinary room,' Kirsty ventured uneasily, feeling on the one hand that she had tricked him and on the other that he just might be patronising her.

'I don't have ordinary rooms,' he muttered vaguely, still enthralled. He crouched down for a closer look and Kirsty had one last try.

'It's very modern. I doubt if it could ever grow in value. I think it——'

'You can stop wriggling.' Adam stood and took out his cheque-book. 'I ordered it, you got it, it's mine. End of subject.' He wrote out a cheque and handed it to her, and Kirsty was still staring at him in a bewildered way when he put it in her hand.

'Shall I wrap it for you?' She was almost whispering, and he tilted her chin with hard fingers.

'Do you show this reluctance to sell with all your clients?' he enquired drily. 'If you try to back out of deals, warn them against purchases and then stand looking stunned when they pay, it's a miracle that you have a thriving establishment.'

'How do you know it thrives?' Kirsty asked, with the same bewildered look about her, and he was back to the sardonic smiles again at once.

'Finance is my business,' he reminded her. 'Why, I actually remember you telling me a long time ago that even your father wouldn't know where to turn if I left.'

It was like being slapped, like a dash of icy water. With one sentence he had thrown her back to four years ago, when she was raging at him. For a few moments she had felt almost in awe of his power and masculine appeal, now she remembered why she hated him, and with that memory came others, memories she could well have managed without.

His hand tightened imperceptibly on her chin and his eyes rested on her lips for another second before he let her go. He was reminding her about that night, reminding her of the way she had simply burst into flame and wound herself close. She could almost feel his lips where his eyes rested, and she couldn't bear it. She turned and walked out of the room.

'Kirsty?' She heard her father's voice, and then Adam's.

'Let her go, Donald. I seem to have offended her, as usual.'

'I can't understand it,' she heard her father mutter as she went up the stairs. 'At one time I thought she loved you more than she loved me.'

'She grew up,' Adam said flatly, and then Kirsty heard no more, but she knew quite well that she had to have a breather before she faced him again, and she rang Guy to see if he would take her out to dinner.

Her father could face those cold, mocking eyes tonight, and when this influx of guests was due she would invite Guy down to prop up her crumbling self-esteem. She knew what Adam was doing. He wanted her out of here, far away, where she would not mention his connection with Selina.

Her father was disappointed that she was going back so soon, but when Kirsty pointed out that she wanted to get the pictures into the gallery and look in on Susan, and that she would be back later anyway, he was somewhat placated. She also found out when the meeting at the house would be during the next week, because she needed this information for Guy.

It was with a feeling of relief that she saw Guy Wentworth come into the restaurant where they had agreed to meet. There was nothing at all threatening about him. He was a broker and he looked the part. He was quiet, reliable and very safe, with none of the flaring good looks of Adam and none of the sensual challenge. She greeted him more warmly than usual, so thankful that she knew him. His stocky build was such a contrast to the lithe, athletic height of Adam, and Guy was so wonderfully ordinary.

'If absence makes the heart grow fonder, then stay away for a while longer.' He laughed as she gave him a very warm hug. 'How long are you staying away, as a matter of interest?' he finished, and Kirsty had to admit that she didn't really know. So far there had been nothing that required a hostess, and after her conversation with her father she was beginning to doubt if there would be more than this meeting that was scheduled for next week.

There was no real reason for her to be staying at the hall, in that case, but she knew that if Adam had not been there she would have been prepared to stay until Selina announced her return. It was wonderful to be in daily contact with her father again, wonderful to be home. Only Adam cast a shadow on things, and she felt a wave of sadness when she remembered how he had brought nothing but happiness to her in the past.

Childhood heroes! How time showed them for what they really were.

She eagerly invited Guy down for dinner on the night the guests were due and by the time she turned her car back to the hall, Kirsty felt she had done all she could to protect herself from Adam's presence.

CHAPTER FOUR

TO HER annoyance he was still there. When she put her head round the study door to say goodnight to her father, she found Adam still firmly established. They were both knee-deep in papers, and it looked as if they had been working for hours. Her father looked tired, and even Adam seemed faintly weary.

'It's time you stopped,' Kirsty stated, looking firmly at her father's tired face. 'Surely nothing can be so pressing that you still have to be up at midnight on a Saturday?'

'We got involved.' Her father rose and ran his hand over his eyes. 'I'm tired out, actually. Lucky you came to order me to bed, Kirsty.'

Adam reached for his jacket, and to Kirsty's great suspicion he didn't even look in her direction.

'Did you have a good time?' her father continued, and Kirsty nodded, her eyes still suspiciously on Adam's bent dark head.

'Yes, we had dinner and then I drove straight back here. I invited Guy down for the dinner on Tuesday, by the way,' she added, more to establish that she was firmly attached to someone than to give her father the information. 'When dinner is over, I imagine you'll be locked up in conversation. It will give me a little time with Guy, because obviously I won't be seeing much of him while I'm here.'

When she looked up, Adam was frowning blackly, his eyes on her face, and it annoyed her that he should resent

61

her guest when this was her home, after all, and her father had simply nodded his approval.

'You have a problem with that?' she asked sharply, but she did not get any sardonic reply. Instead, Adam just shrugged indifferently.

'Is it any of my business? If I look displeased I can assure you that it's just that I suddenly realise how late it is and how tired I am. I walked up here from the lodge. Now I have to walk back.'

'Stay here for the night,' her father suggested, and Kirsty was amazed at the burst of consternation that shot through her.

Before she knew what she was saying she had blurted out, 'My car is still at the door. I'll drive you down to the lodge. It's no trouble.'

Adam looked startled and her father gave her a quick kiss of approval.

'Kind girl,' he muttered. 'I'll have to get off to bed or I'll fall down.' He walked out, and Kirsty found Adam still staring at her.

'Is this kindness going to kill me?' he enquired, and Kirsty bristled at the words.

'It was just a charitable gesture. If you'd rather walk, however...'

'Not at this time of night. I'm dropping too,' he muttered. 'I'll take this gesture at face value and mull it over tomorrow, when I have my wits back.'

In the car, Kirsty reflected that if the kindly gesture killed anyone it would probably be her. She was much too aware that Adam was beside her. His presence seemed to be filling her small car and she knew it was only panic at the idea of his staying at the hall overnight that had prompted this act of charity. He would probably have refused, in any case.

It was mad, and it would have been quite simple to offer the loan of her car until morning. Instead of that she was now driving down to the lodge under the giant trees that edged the drive, with a silent and probably thoughtful man beside her and the air singing with questions and suspicion. She was greatly pleased to be able to stop at the lodge and wish him a brief goodnight.

He did not answer, and as she turned to him to say goodnight again, and speed him on his way, he looked at her levelly.

'OK,' he announced darkly. 'I fathomed it out. You panicked at the idea of my staying overnight at the hall. You imagined I would creep up on you in the early hours, Kirsty?'

'I don't like this conversation, please go,' Kirsty said quickly, but he just ignored her.

'I should perhaps remind you that, had I any such inclination, I had a good opportunity four years ago, when you clung to me so feverishly and kissed me back with an astonishing enthusiasm.'

'Get out of my car!' Kirsty snapped, glad of the darkness that hid her hot face from his penetrating gaze. 'If you don't, then I'll get out and walk back myself.'

'And you know perfectly well that I won't let you.' She glared at him and opened the car door, ready to step out, but she got nowhere at all because Adam's hand came to her arm, restraining her. 'I'm going,' he assured her.

He looked at her for a second before opening his own door and preparing to leave. 'How did we get to be like this with each other, Kirsty?' he said softly, and she turned her face away as she reached forward to restart the car.

'What did you expect?' she asked bitterly. 'Did you imagine I would go on following you around and worshipping you when you took up with Selina?'

'Yes, there's the matter of Selina,' he agreed quietly. 'I sometimes quite forget that you know all about that after a bit of schoolgirl snooping.'

'I was not snooping!' Kirsty spun round at him. 'It was a complete accident, and something I just didn't want to know,' she finished in a choked voice, turning her head away.

'Because you worshipped me?' He turned her face back, but she refused to look at him.

'Yes, I did,' she whispered. 'You were everything in my life and then, quite suddenly, you were nothing. Everything I believed in vanished overnight.'

'So you refused university and even gave up art school,' he surmised quietly. 'It went on hurting so much, Kirsty?'

'I wasn't hurt. I was shocked,' she managed defiantly. 'When an idol falls there are repercussions. As I was the only one who knew, the backlash was all mine.'

She refused to meet his eyes, but she knew he was watching her, and she waited for the excuses, the denials. None came.

'Goodnight, angel-face.' He simply got out of the car and walked away, and Kirsty swung round fast and drove back to the hall, wiping impatiently at the tears on her cheeks, furiously glad that he didn't know how much it had hurt her.

Her father had said that he had thought she loved Adam more than himself, and how right he had been. She had loved Adam. He had been the very centre of her life. He had just called her angel-face, another thing from the past. Tears fell faster, and she realised that she had never mourned the loss of Adam. She had been angry, felt betrayed, but she had bottled it up and now, with a few words, he had released the whole thing. Yes, she had loved him, and he was quite, quite gone.

After that, Kirsty planned things differently. The burst of tears had somehow started the healing, and she could now face Adam each evening and make bright, interesting conversation without being afraid to look at him. When she did look at him she saw Selina, she saw them together, and her face showed moments of scorn that he did not fail to notice.

Adam, too, had a different attitude. The sarcastic comments were few and far between and he seemed to be much more quiet. A certain amount of tension had drained away but they were left as strangers, polite strangers, trying to get through this time without discord. Suddenly both of them seemed to be behaving within textbook rules of good breeding, and Donald Sinclair was clearly puzzled. They both wanted him to be kept out of things but their reasons were entirely different. Kirsty's reasons were for the love of her father. Adam's reasons were despicable.

The day of the dinner party dawned, and, as she had already made it quite clear to Mrs Drew that she was in charge, Kirsty expected no trouble at all. And, of course, Guy would be there, although by now she did not feel quite so much in need of protection. Adam's cold courtesy was no threat and Kirsty's only worry was that everything should go smoothly.

By the time the first guests arrived she knew that things would be all right. The caterers had been on time. Mrs Drew was being frostily efficient and Kirsty had spent a long time getting ready. It was the first time in her life that she had acted as hostess for her father and it would have to be instinct that guided her. She had none of Selina's polish. All she could do was give it her best shot.

There were ten men, no women, and Kirsty was glad of that. Taking coffee with a bunch of unknown females was not her style. When the business discussions got underway, she could disappear into the sitting-room with Guy and get her breath back.

She seemed to be flying around in all directions, and although she had been introduced to every guest as they arrived she had not the faintest idea as to who they really were. Adam was not yet there and her father was holding the fort alone, not that it mattered. People were standing around in the drawing-room with drinks and already, as far as she could see, business was all they were talking about.

When Guy was shown in she almost ran across to him. Without him she knew she would be sitting at the dinner table with no conversation at all. They were going to discuss mergers and assets, and that left her with her mouth open.

'You look gorgeous,' Guy whispered into her ear as she gave him a welcoming hug. He kissed her cheek and then drew back to look her over. 'Fit to eat,' he pronounced.

She was pleased, because she had taken a lot of trouble for this evening. In the first place, her shining, nut-brown hair was swept up and pinned at the back, the closest to sophistication she could get. Her gown was a softly shimmering lilac colour, sweeping down from a halter-neck, and she had deliberately worn no jewellery at all. The very simplicity was eye-catching and she felt good, sure of herself—until she saw Adam.

He came in a few seconds after Guy, just as she was smiling into Guy's satisfied-looking face, and as she was turned in that direction, she noticed him at once. He saw her too, and she supposed it was not surprising that his eyes fell on her, as she was the only woman in the room. His glance lanced over her and the cool indifference on his face really stung.

It actually hurt that he did not give her the admiring looks that she had received from all the other men as they arrived, and Kirsty fought down the feeling as she turned Guy to be introduced.

'This is Adam Frazer, my father's partner,' she said pleasantly, 'and this is Guy Wentworth.' She noted that the handshake was very brief. Adam's eyes went round the room after his curt nod of acknowledgement to Guy, and for a second she thought he was about to walk off without saying anything at all.

'I see the gang's all here,' he murmured sardonically. 'Get me a drink, Kirsty, will you? If I go over there I'll be knee-deep in finance before I've even eaten my soup.'

Kirsty had no alternative. She was supposed to be the hostess here, but it meant leaving him with Guy, and suddenly she was uneasy again. There was a menace about Adam this evening that had been absent for the past few days, and she almost spilled the drink as she hurried back to them.

'Perfect,' Adam said, taking the glass from her hand. 'I can guarantee you'll always know exactly what I want.' He smiled down at her, towering over her, overshadowing Guy, and she was looking up at him with great suspicion when he continued, 'Have you told your friend how far back we go, angel?'

'Er—Adam is an old family friend,' Kirsty managed quickly. She was beginning to feel scared, because she couldn't understand what Adam was up to but everything about him spelled quiet trouble. He was being possessive, and speaking almost as if Guy wasn't there at all.

'Kirsty, come and do your duty.' Her father appeared and collected her, making her join the bigger group, and she couldn't help looking anxiously over her shoulder as she left. She had no idea what Adam would say when she wasn't there, and the tension that had not been present for the past few days came back, especially as when she looked round Adam smiled at her like a watching tiger.

All through dinner the feeling grew. Every time she looked up Adam was watching her, and he seemed to be capable of holding two conversations at once and never taking his eyes off her in the meantime. She berated herself for falling into the trap of complacency. She had known from the first that he was going to be dangerous, and yet she had almost wilfully relaxed over the past few days.

When the business discussions got underway after dinner she was almost hysterically glad to escape to the small sitting-room with Guy, although by now she couldn't think of anything to say at all.

'That's a clever chap,' Guy remarked as he sat down comfortably with his coffee. 'Enough intelligence to be alarming. I've met similar people before in my line of work, but no one quite like him.'

'Who?' Kirsty asked distractedly, knowing perfectly well who he was talking about. Who could pick out somebody else when Adam was there?

'Frazer,' Guy stated, giving her a quizzical look. 'He told me he'd known you since you were a child. You never mentioned him to me.'

'He—er—I haven't seen him for years, until recently. I never even thought about him.'

'I would have imagined he'd be impossible to forget,' Guy murmured drily. 'He's certainly striking to look at.' He watched her for a minute and then said quietly, 'He had an attitude about you—vigilant. There's something between you both, isn't there?'

'Only animosity,' Kirsty assured him. She didn't want to talk about Adam because suddenly it was hurting again. It was all right letting the past out and thinking that one small burst of weeping would wash it away. All that had happened was that she had been left feeling vulnerable, because the anger she had lived on for years was not now so readily available.

'He never took his eyes off you from the moment he arrived,' Guy insisted, and Kirsty felt very tired of all this. She went out with Guy, liked him. He kissed her goodnight and held her hand but it had gone no further, and suddenly she knew that she had never wanted it to go further. He was stepping into a battle he knew nothing about. It was her problem, and Adam's.

With that thought came another. Even after so long, bitterness held them together, just as affection had held them together before. She was not at all free from Adam and the thought devastated her.

'Adam and I go back a long way,' she said wearily. 'There are—family problems that we both have to deal with. Just don't get the wrong idea.'

'He's got a very possessive air about him when he speaks of you.'

'What did he say?' Kirsty's head shot up, anxiety sweeping over her, and that was when the tension really hit her, and she felt the stab of pain in her head that she had not felt for years.

'Not much,' Guy assured her. 'Just the odd little thing. I couldn't put my finger on it but I got the feeling he was warning me off, very politely.'

'You're quite mistaken,' Kirsty insisted, and he gave her another wry look.

'He called you angel.'

'I've known him all my life, almost. It was a throw-back to the past.' A deliberate throw-back, she knew, and another thing from the past was rapidly catching up on her. The pain in her head was growing, and when she looked at Guy there were lights around him, partly obscuring his face.

'What's wrong?' he asked in a suddenly alert voice. 'You're like a ghost. If I've upset you with prying...'

'It's migraine,' Kirsty said shakily. 'I haven't had it for years—clearly I'm not up to this hostess business.'

'Tell me what to do.' Guy was on his feet at once, but she shook her head, gasping with the growing pain.

'You can't do anything. I have to go to bed. Oh, Guy, I'm so sorry, really I am. It's not been a very good evening for you.'

'It seems to have been a worse evening for you,' he muttered. 'I've brought all this on with my jealous probing.'

'Honestly, you haven't,' Kirsty assured him, adding thoughtlessly, 'If anybody caused it, it was Adam.'

'You love him, don't you?' he asked quietly, and she looked at him through pain-filled eyes.

'I did once, when I was a child. Now I hate him and he hates me. He's just trouble. After these two weeks I'll not see him again.'

She went with Guy into the hall to see him out, guilt about him making her feel even worse. She knew she could not even go in to see her father and explain her absence. She would just have to creep away. Even now she wanted to hang on to Guy's arm for support. As they were almost at the front door Adam appeared, his glance shooting over her.

'What's wrong?' He was beside her immediately, and Guy answered for her before she could speak. In fact, it was getting more difficult to speak by the second.

'Migraine,' Guy said coldly, giving Adam a look of dislike that was utterly ignored.

'Damn! I thought you'd got rid of that,' Adam muttered, turning her pale face to the light. She winced and he let her drop her head, but he kept his hand warmly on her nape. 'Well, you're not faking it this time.' He glanced at Guy. 'Can you see yourself out? She has to go to bed.'

'I'm not a child,' Kirsty protested weakly, hearing the possessive tone that Guy had heard earlier. His hand was slowly massaging her nape, warm and tempting. She wanted to lean against him and be comforted.

'Just a nuisance,' Adam muttered, grasping her shoulder with his free hand and pulling her back against him as she made a move towards Guy.

'It's all right, Kirsty,' Guy assured her. 'I'll phone you.'

'You don't understand——' she began almost tearfully. She could hear how Adam sounded, and Guy didn't know that he was simply paying her back for knowing about Selina.

'Forget it, love,' Guy muttered. He came and kissed her cheek, manfully ignoring Adam's presence. 'I'll phone you. Go to bed.'

He went, and Kirsty wriggled free of Adam's grasp and turned to the stairs. The desire to stay as she was, her back pressed against the warmth of his body, was too tempting, and she was still worrying about the evening.

'I let everyone down,' she murmured painfully. 'I'm a flop as a hostess on my very first attempt and I've practically thrown Guy out after inviting him here. Now I'm sneaking off.'

'You were bright and beautiful,' Adam said firmly from just behind her. 'Your elegance established the tone of the evening. That was all that was required. Your father will manage without you and it was about time your friend left anyway.'

'He's my boyfriend,' Kirsty said piteously, wanting it established even if it wasn't true, but Adam urged her to the stairs, his hand warmly against her back.

'Fancy that,' he exclaimed sarcastically. 'It never occurred to me. Get to bed. He's safely out of reach.'

She wanted to stop and argue, but she knew she wasn't up to it, and she suspected he would not have allowed it in any case. She urgently needed to lie down, but when she reached the stairs Kirsty knew she had left things too long. She couldn't climb them and she stopped, her head bent in defeat.

'I can't do it,' she muttered weakly. 'The stairs are too much. I'll fall down.'

'You little fool,' Adam growled, swinging her up into his arms. 'Why didn't you act before this? What were you trying to prove? You only had to call me.'

'It hit me suddenly.' She shivered and he held her more closely, steadily climbing the stairs to her room. It was so long since he had held her, and the comfort made her feel unutterably sad. It was like a glimpse of something that had left a faint wistfulness behind from long ago. She wanted to cling to him, to shout that it wasn't fair. He had said that she'd only had to call him. If only it were that simple. She glanced up at him, and she could only see part of his face by now. The migraine had really taken hold.

'I can't see you, Adam,' she whispered mournfully, and he looked down into her white face.

'Imagine me, then,' he suggested quietly. 'I haven't changed much. I'm still the same. I'd got over my adolescent traumas long before I met you. You're the only one with a problem.'

'All I have is migraine.'

'And a stubborn determination to see me in hell. That's where the migraine came from. You're playing out of your league.'

He sounded cold again, disinterested, and Kirsty stopped trying to cope; she put her head to his shoulder and suffered quietly. Just for a minute. Nothing mattered but the comfort he was giving her. If he had walked on forever it would have been all right with her.

In her room he put her on the bed after glancing round with impatience. 'A pale girl in a pale room,' he murmured disparagingly. 'Virginal simplicity.'

'Only because the room hasn't been changed,' Kirsty muttered defensively. 'I've changed.'

Adam looked down at her coldly. 'An experienced woman of the world,' he sneered. 'No wonder he left so readily if he only has to wait.'

Kirsty had brought that on herself, but she wasn't capable of following through.

'Thank you for bringing me up here,' she said weakly. 'I can manage.'

'You're not getting the chance,' he grated. 'Where are your tablets?'

'I haven't had any for years. I used to keep them in the bathroom cabinet but they might have been thrown out.'

'And if they haven't they'll probably be useless,' Adam snapped, striding to her bathroom. 'You never seem to be prepared for anything!'

She had to agree that she was never prepared for Adam. She could hear him rummaging about, but she had now sunk to the pillows, the light unbearable on her eyes. When he came back in she tried to look at him; he was reading the label on a box.

'They'll do,' he said briefly. 'I'll get you a glass of water.'

He sounded so angry that Kirsty wished he was miles away, and when he came back she swallowed the tablets and sank back to the bed.

'Get undressed,' he ordered sharply, and tears came to the edge of her lashes.

'Just go away!' she choked. 'I've got enough trouble without listening to you raging at me.'

'I am not raging. I merely want to see you comfortably settled, and you're not helping much.'

'Neither are you, snarling away like that!' The tears escaped and slid to her cheeks from her closed eyes, and she heard him mutter under his breath before she felt his hands lifting her up.

'It's self-defence. When confused and under attack, an animal snarls.' His voice softened. 'Come on, you poor little creature. Get out of this fabulous dress.'

'Did—did you think it was fabulous?' Kirsty asked miserably, peering up at him. 'You didn't look as if you did.'

'You're rambling,' Adam warned. 'Say nothing more, because you'll regret it later and take it out on me.' He took the pins out of her hair, letting it fall back to her shoulders, his fingers running lightly through it. 'Yes,' he continued softly, 'you looked fabulous, Kirsty. I noticed.'

He unfastened the halter-top of her dress, and it suddenly dawned on Kirsty that she had no slip on underneath. It hadn't been possible. She was just letting Adam do anything.

'Stop!' she gasped with shaky urgency. 'I have to do it myself.'

His glance swept over her and she could still see well enough to notice the way he summed things up. His hands lingered warmly on her shoulders for a second and then he turned his back.

'All right, but I'm not leaving until you're safely in bed. Tell me when you're decent.'

It was hard to move fast but she tried, and she had just struggled into her nightie when the door opened without so much as a knock and Mrs Drew stood there, clean towels in her hands. For a second they were both too startled to speak and Mrs Drew took advantage of the situation, looking knowingly from one to the other.

'I brought clean towels, Miss Sinclair. I imagined that everyone was downstairs. I had no idea you were here.'

Kirsty's pale face flushed at the tone, but matters were taken out of her hands.

'And no recollection of how to knock on a door,' Adam grated before Kirsty could speak. 'Do you normally barge into bedrooms without knocking, or is this some special occasion?'

'Normally, when there is a gathering at the house, people stay downstairs——' Mrs Drew began, her face reddening at Adam's words, and he stared at her with far more frost than she could ever summon up.

'One knocks on bedroom doors, Mrs Drew,' he interrupted coldly. 'It's a behaviour pattern that I suggest you follow in future. This is no longer an empty room in the house. Miss Sinclair has come home. This is her room.'

Mrs Drew just put the towels on the chest by the door and almost fled, and Adam grunted angrily. It was obvious what she had thought, and it was just one more upsetting thing.

'Get rid of her,' he snapped. 'That woman is a menace.'

'She'll report this to Selina,' Kirsty surmised thoughtlessly, and then cried out in fright as Adam lifted her from the bed by her arms and crushed her against him with a fury that she had never expected.

'Shut up!' he snarled. 'One more word and I'll forget what a pitiful object you are at this moment!' He stared down at her and his anger did not ease, even when he saw the tears which still clung to her dark lashes. She was wincing with pain, unable to make any move to struggle free, and she gave a small moan of anguish as he clasped her head and kissed her with a suppressed fury that forced her lips apart.

When he let her go she was shaking, more tears on her face, and he lifted her into bed, sweeping the dress away and covering her with the sheets.

'Now, close your eyes and go to sleep,' he ordered forcefully, 'and just be thankful that you're in this pathetic condition, because you're in the right place to be taught a lesson, virginal room or not!'

He draped her dress over a chair and turned off the lamps before heading for the door. She was still trying to see him as he opened it and spun round to glare at her.

'One of these days, I'm going to lose my self-control and either kill or cure you, Kirsty!' he rasped through clenched teeth. He closed the door none too quietly and Kirsty lay in pain, waiting for the tablets to take effect. If they didn't she would have to call for her father. No, she wouldn't have to do that, she corrected. Adam would be telling him right now, after he had got his temper under control.

Her lips were still stinging and she ran her tongue round them carefully. He was a brute. She turned on her side and felt great relief as the tablets began to act. She couldn't think any more. In the morning she would think. Adam would not be there, and it would be possible to consider things in a more rational light. Right at this moment he had too many advantages, not the least of which being her pitiful reliance on him, and her worrying knowledge that she had been glad it was Adam looking after her and not anyone else.

It was two days before Kirsty felt really well again, and during that time Adam kept completely away. According to her father, he had gone back to London to take a close look at the renovations to his own place, and after that he would have to go down to Eastbourne.

At least it gave Kirsty time to collect her somewhat scattered thoughts and prepare herself for seeing him again. Probably the Eastbourne trip would be extended, while he flew across to Paris and met Selina, she thought bitterly.

'When is Selina coming back?' she asked her father, and he just shrugged, almost without interest.

'I have no idea. She hasn't even telephoned. It's not unusual. When she gets to these places she thinks of nothing but clothes. I just pick up the bills.'

His amused indifference made Kirsty realise how far from him she had really been. Selina's boutiques must be paying well, but her father was still footing the bill. He had helped Kirsty set up the gallery, and backed her until she got going, but she had insisted on paying every penny back. Selina had no such qualms. She wanted everything, and she was still getting away with it.

It was good to have a couple of days alone with her father, though, to be able to potter around the estate without the possibility of meeting Adam, and her father had sheepishly admitted that the meeting that had been held at the house was the only one arranged. He had simply wanted her home.

Well, she would stay. Susan was managing perfectly well and, although she would have to call in at the gallery during the week, she was happy enough here until Selina came back.

Kirsty went down to London a few days later and spent a happy morning rearranging pictures, talking to Susan and doing the books. The setter was on its way to America and her customer had collected the husky, delighted with it, according to her assistant. She was almost ready to go when someone came in, and Susan hurried forward to help them.

Kirsty felt like hiding in a corner, because as soon as he spoke she knew that it was Adam and he was asking for her. There was nothing for it but to appear, and he stood watching her as she came down the steps from her flat. His eyes skimmed over her. She knew she had lost a couple of pounds while she had been struck down by the migraine, but it didn't require such a close inspection.

'Buying or browsing?' she enquired pertly, and was glad to see an almost normal smile.

'Looking for help,' he corrected. 'Donald told me you were here when I rang. I want some help with the panther.'

'What have you done with it?' Kirsty asked sharply. 'You've surely not let it get damaged? That picture is a beauty, and even if you don't want it after all——'

'Hold everything!' Adam ordered. 'Small wonder you get so tense. You immediately imagine the worst. The panther is fine. I want your opinion on where to hang it.'

'I just sell pictures,' Kirsty said stiffly, suspicion raising its head at once, and he glanced round the long room.

'And place them to perfection,' he finished wryly. 'Look, I paid a thousand for that panther, and I think you could spare me a few minutes to suggest the exact spot.'

Over his shoulder Kirsty could see Susan's face, her expression priceless. She was silently mouthing the word 'thousand', and then, with raised eyebrows, 'pounds?'. Kirsty felt her lips twitching, and Adam noticed at once.

'You're in a good mood,' he surmised. 'I couldn't have come at a better time. Take pity on me.' He stood looking at her and Kirsty saw for the first time in years that the grey eyes had turned smokily dark. It struck at her heart. He had been so very dear to her, so greatly adored. It just wasn't fair that things had gone so hopelessly wrong. Even now, when he looked like that, she was defenceless.

'All right,' she said huskily. 'I'll come, but I'm not staying long. I'm going back home.'

'I'll drive you back,' Adam offered quietly, his eyes alert on her downcast face, but she pulled herself together and met his gaze.

'I drove down. Naturally, I'll be driving myself back.'

He nodded thoughtfully. 'Fair enough. We'll go in convoy. I'm impatient to get back myself. That lodge is starting to feel like home, and, in any case, there's the same old magic about the estate.'

Kirsty knew what he meant. There *was* a magic about Parbury Hall, about the beautiful grounds, the tall trees and the river. It was something she had been forced to give up for Selina. She had given Adam up for her too.

'Let's go,' she said briskly, her smile dying away. 'I'll follow you, but don't get too far away. I have no idea where you live.'

She turned for a quick last word with Susan, and Adam waited for her at the door, his expression thoughtful again. When she came, he went to his car without a word, and Kirsty once again berated herself. She should not have allowed him to persuade her into this. It was quite mad. She had not the faintest desire to know where he lived or how he lived. She wanted nothing to do with him, because there was no way he would be allowed to hurt her again.

CHAPTER FIVE

ADAM lived in a very modern block right in the centre of town, and Kirsty was astonished. Not many minutes ago he had been talking of the magic of Parbury Hall, and now he was taking her to the penthouse apartment of a towering steel construction.

'I thought you liked being at Parbury,' she said as they zoomed up in a high-speed lift. 'There's not much magic here.'

'If I can't have the magic I want then I prefer something modern and cool,' Adam said shortly. 'A townhouse with a garden doesn't appeal.'

He unlocked the door as they reached the top of the building and led her inside, and it was certainly a shock. It was starkly modern, the sort of place she imagined an architect would like to own. Even though they had entered a very large hall they had not reached the living quarters, and Adam motioned to some stairs.

'Up here,' he said. 'I like to live above things. It gives me a good deal of satisfaction to peer down at the world.'

'I thought you always peered down at the world,' Kirsty murmured, looking around her. 'You don't need any sort of advantage.'

'Is that a compliment, I wonder?' he queried, showing her into an enormous room with great picture windows that looked out over the city.

London seemed to be spread out below them. The view was remarkable, but Kirsty didn't look for more than a second. She was too intrigued by the room itself. The walls were white and two great white settees with dark tables beside them were the main items of furniture. The simplicity was awesome, and even the addition of lacquered cabinets and modern hi-fi equipment did nothing to detract from the fact that everything had been kept to the very minimum.

'And you said I had a virginal room?' Kirsty muttered, and got herself a quizzical look.

'I thought at the time that it suited you,' he said shortly. 'However, you disposed of that particular idea rapidly.' He glanced round. 'This is the very opposite of everything that I found when I first went to Parbury Hall. I think perhaps it's a sort of rebellion.'

'An efficient removal of magic,' Kirsty surmised. 'And yet—it could be quite beautiful.'

'Are you going to make it beautiful for me?' His question had Kirsty turning away, squashing her ideas quickly. She would never allow herself to be drawn into his life again.

'It has nothing to do with me,' she assured him briskly. 'I don't even want to be here. This visit is just a sort of professional courtesy.'

'Then I'll make you a coffee while you wander round and decide about the panther's resting place.'

He walked out to another room, and Kirsty bit into her lip with vexation. He always had been able to get to her. Now she was almost feeling sorry for him because he couldn't have the magic he wanted. She put her hands in her pockets and wandered round the room.

It certainly needed pictures. She had the feeling that he had just had it redecorated like this. It almost looked as if it had been done in a fit of rage, or something akin to it.

She was still standing, contemplating things, when he came back with two steaming mugs of coffee, and she took hers almost absent-mindedly, leaning back against the rail that guarded the drop to the hall.

'What was it like before you had it redecorated?' she enquired, and he shot her an almost wary glance.

'How do you know it wasn't the same as this?' he asked, and she shrugged, glancing around the room.

'I don't know—instinct, perhaps? There's a sort of feeling—anger? Frustration? I'm not at all sure, but you haven't had something done that... Oh, I don't know!' She gave a small embarrassed laugh. 'It's probably imagination.'

He was sitting on the settee facing her, his eyes skimming over her troubled face, and she pulled herself together sharply. She was being normal, talking almost intimately to him. It was useless to do that, and she began to roam around again, looking for the right spot.

'Behind you,' she decided finally. 'Right in the centre of that wall.' She grimaced and looked at him quizzically. 'It would take everything I have at the gallery to do anything at all for this room.'

'Then, collect things for me,' he suggested quietly, and she looked back at him, searching for sarcasm and finding none at all.

'Not a collection, as such,' she insisted. 'You need a good variety here.' She looked around and then turned away abruptly, putting her coffee down unfinished. 'You shouldn't be here,' she said impatiently. 'It's not you. It—it's not even happy.' She turned to face him with a frown. 'Why are you doing this to yourself?'

He stood slowly and walked towards her.

'How very astute you grew up to be,' he complimented her quietly. 'Why am I doing this? Probably rebellion, as I told you, or, much more likely, bloody-mindedness. If I can't have my own particular magic, then I don't want any at all!'

'Then look for your magic,' Kirsty insisted, and he smiled down at her.

'It's unattainable. Somewhere along the line it slipped through my fingers.'

It sounded so final, so sad, that Kirsty felt it hit her deep inside, and her green eyes searched his face. 'Don't stay here, Adam,' she pleaded. 'Finally it will hurt you.'

His lips twisted in a peculiar smile and he reached out to touch her face. 'At the moment, it's fine. You and I are right at the top of the world in a room with no past and no future. What could be better?'

His eyes were drawing her to him irresistibly, and almost without thinking Kirsty moved closer, to be gathered into his arms and brought against the warmth of his body. His eyes were smokily grey again, and she stared into his face with a sort of entrancing look about her that widened his smile.

'Angel-face,' he murmured, and then his night-dark head bent to hers and she found herself meeting his lips with an eagerness that she knew was nothing short of madness.

He was kissing her gently, his caresses soothing, but she didn't want to be soothed. She wanted to make things better for him, and she wound her arms around his neck with no hesitation. He brought her even closer, and as soon as she felt his body against hers Kirsty melted completely, no other thought in her mind but the feeling of being near to him.

Like that time four years ago, the wild fire started to grow, and when she tightened her arms round his neck his kisses turned to flame too, and he lowered her to the white settee and back into his arms. She could feel the heat coming from him, she could touch the warmth of his skin, and Kirsty forgot the past.

He trailed heated kisses over her face and neck, holding her away when she wanted badly to kiss him back, but when his hand cupped her breast through the softness of her sweater she gave an impatient cry and pulled his head down to hers, her lips meeting his with the same fervour she had shown so long ago.

'Kirsty,' he whispered, his tongue circling her lips, and she opened her mouth, ardently accepting the fierce invasion. His tongue moved almost secretly in the dark warmth of her mouth, and Kirsty felt an ache grow inside her that seemed to spread all over. Her fingers clutched at his hair and she pulled his head closer, urgently kissing him until their breathing was a harsh sound in the silence of the room.

When he slid her sweater over her head and bent to trail his lips across her skin she arched against him fervently, her legs parting to bring him closer, her fingers tearing at the buttons of his shirt, even while her mind was shocked by the way she was reacting to him.

Dear heaven! How had she come to this from her uneasy pacing about of not so long ago? He only had to look closely at her and she went to him. She never wanted to be anywhere else but right here, lost in the sensual fire that burned both of them. She never wanted anyone but Adam to touch her for the rest of her life.

'Adam!' She cried his name frustratedly, and he tore his shirt over his head, looking down at her, his eyes absorbed by the beauty of her breasts. He lowered himself slowly over her, the dark hair on his chest tingling against her, and she tossed her head back wantonly, her little cries urging him on.

'I want you, Kirsty,' he muttered thickly. 'You're driving me mad.'

She felt the zip of her skirt plunge down and then it was tossed free, and the warmth of Adam's hand was sending a yearning pain deep inside her. She moved against him excitedly and he crushed her beneath him, his hand moving to trace her legs with the heat that spoke of his commitment.

'You're mine, Kirsty!' he said almost violently. 'Look at me! Let me see what those green eyes are saying.'

And she opened her eyes, their green depths dazed with feeling, her gaze encountering the heated darkness of his. He looked almost cruel, his face strained, his eyes narrowed and watchful.

She moved frustratedly and he smiled, a slow twisting of his lips.

'You want me, angel?' he asked huskily, but she didn't answer, all she did was reach out anxiously, to pull him back down to her, her mind too dazed even to consider the low sound of triumph he made deep in his throat.

He gathered her against him, his lips claiming hers again, and they were soaring back into the wild heat that they seemed to generate when the telephone rang. Adam ignored it, and Kirsty was too dazzled by her feelings to even give it a moment's thought, but it continued harshly, stridently intruding into the sensuous world that surrounded them, and finally it could be ignored no longer.

Adam swore softly and rolled over to pick it up, and Kirsty felt cold and lost. As soon as he left her there was fear, and she longed to reach out for him, to knock the telephone to the floor and beg for the world they had just left. Suddenly she didn't have him any more and everything was different; the old forlorn feeling was back.

'Hello?' Adam grated with little courtesy, and then his face set in a grim look that warned Kirsty of trouble. 'I'm busy,' he snapped, 'and Paris is a long way off. At this moment of no interest to me at all.' He listened for a while and then bit out, 'Maybe you do, but that's your problem. Phone Donald and see what he thinks.'

He had to listen for a few more seconds, but that was all the time Kirsty needed to slip into her skirt and pull her sweater over her head, and by the time he slammed the phone down she was across the room, making for the stairs.

'Kirsty!' He sounded stricken, bewildered, but she knew who had been at the other end of that call, she could almost make up the rest of the conversation. Selina had been wanting him to go to Paris but he had been busy right at that moment—busy with her!

'Don't come near me!' Kirsty shouted, pointing a threatening finger at him as he got to his feet. He looked white and shaken, and she could well imagine that he was. She was pretty shaken herself. 'You bastard!' she raged bitterly. 'Phone her back! It's a short flight to Paris!'

'Kirsty, you don't understand——' he began, but she had heard enough, and she almost fell down the stairs in her haste to be away from him.

'I understand. Just keep away from me,' she threatened. 'Come within an inch of me again and I'll tell my father everything I should have told him years ago!'

She slammed out of the flat and went down in the lift, almost running to her car, and it was not until she was very close to home that the realisation of where she had been heading with Adam hit her hard. It hit her so hard that she had to pull into the side of the road and rest her head against the steering-wheel.

She had been equally to blame. She had never, ever behaved like that, but she only had to be near Adam to want to be overwhelmed by him. She felt nothing but disgust with herself, and it was made worse by the fact that she also felt regret. She wanted him so badly that it was a pain inside her that refused to stop.

Things were now completely different, and Kirsty knew she could no longer stay at the hall. Her promise would have to be broken, because she could not contemplate sitting down to dinner each night and facing Adam. She would give herself a few minutes to recover when she got back and then she would break the news to her father. It would be fairly easy to come up with an excuse.

She did not need an excuse, as it turned out, because as she came into the house her father met her, with the news that Adam would not be coming for a while.

'He's going to Portugal. We've got a big contract there and Adam thinks the people on the spot are being less than competent. He doesn't like to see money drifting away into a bottomless hole. By the time he's finished with them, they'll be razor-sharp efficient.' He grinned at her. 'I'd love to be there. I've seen him in action before. He just appears quietly and feathers fly.'

'A dangerous hunter,' Kirsty muttered, and her father laughed.

'He's a bit like that. He never raises his voice, but people fall about trying to explain themselves. I don't know how I ever managed without Adam.' He put his arm round her shoulders. 'Anyway, he's almost like a son by now. In many ways, he's family. You know that, darling.'

Kirsty could have wept. When her father found out about Adam and Selina it would break his heart. She hoped he would not be trying to contact Adam in

Portugal either, because he would not be there very long. The whole reason for the trip was the phone call from Selina. He was going to Paris. He had snapped at Selina on the phone because she had interrupted, but he would be going all the same.

Kirsty made an excuse and went to her room as the thought of that deepened. If the telephone had not rung she would by now have been a different person. She should have been grateful to Selina, but she shivered when she admitted that she was not grateful at all. For those wild minutes she had wanted to belong to Adam, and her stomach clenched with pain when she thought of it. She must never see him again. This was the last time she could ever come home.

Over the next few days she divided her time between Parbury Hall and her gallery. There was nothing to occupy her when her father went to the office and she had more to do than hang around and watch Mrs Drew. Since Adam had savaged the housekeeper she had been more frosty than ever, obviously biding her time until Selina came back, but she had also been scrupulously polite. She really was a thorn in the flesh, and Kirsty could have done without a sight of her.

Each morning as her father left for work Kirsty left also, after discussing dinner with Mrs Drew, and it was always a great relief to step into the quiet of her own place of work. She needed the silence of her own flat for at least some time of the day, because she could never be at Parbury Hall without thinking of Adam.

As she was always home at night, to be with her father, she met Guy for lunch on several occasions, and he had the good sense not to mention the dinner party and the events that had taken place. What she would have done if he had brought up the subject, Kirsty did not know. Adam's face was rarely out of her mind. Things had changed, and her anger now was more the painful lashing out of some deeply hurt creature than the scornful disdain she had felt before.

By the time the next Friday came around she had almost managed to force herself back into normality. She had been to a sale during the day and the excitement of that had helped, although she had let herself be carried away by buying two landscapes and a surrealist picture on the spur of the moment.

It had almost been an act committed under hypnosis, because she had no use for them at all. They were for Adam's apartment and she knew it. Somehow she had not been able to help herself. The stark vision of that place had stuck in her mind, and over and over she had reorganised it, reshaped it, in a mental exercise that was solely to keep her mind from his face.

When she got back to the gallery she left them in the car, once again hiding her instinctive desire to get Adam anything he needed. What he needed was Selina, and as Kirsty took her more usual purchases in, to discuss them with Susan, she was once more berating herself for her own foolish actions.

It had made her a little late too, and she only had time to change her clothes and do her face again before she had to rush off for lunch with Guy. She would not be coming to London over the weekend and it was the last time she would see him until the following week.

When she got to the restaurant where they had arranged to meet, Guy was already there. As she walked in he stood and signalled to her, his eyes admiring, but the brilliant smile that Kirsty gave him began to fade as she felt other eyes on her. It was almost as if someone was willing her to look at them, a feeling so strong that it could not be ignored. She turned her head slightly and her smile faded away completely, because sitting a few feet away from the table where she would be eating her lunch was Adam.

He was with two other men and she knew it would be a business lunch, but it was uncanny that they should have ended up here. Guy had taken her to a different restaurant every day and the sheer coincidence of meeting Adam was like a cruel destiny. For a second she just stopped, her eyes wide and distressed, but Adam showed no sign at all of recognition.

He stared at her with cold, grey eyes, looking at her as if she were a stranger, and it was only the feel of Guy's hand on her arm that broke the icy spell.

'Sit down, Kirsty,' Guy urged quietly. 'Whatever it is, don't just stand there.'

'I'm sorry.' Kirsty allowed him to see her to her chair, and she was thankful to find that she was not able to see Adam once she was seated. He was somewhere behind her, and although she could still feel his eyes burning into her she didn't have to look at him.

'I observe that things have got worse between you two,' Guy murmured wryly. He looked closely at her pale face. 'We can go and eat elsewhere if you like.'

'No!' Kirsty looked up at him fiercely. 'He's not making me run. I'm perfectly fine, thank you.'

'Then let's order and ignore him,' Guy suggested in a comfortable voice, and Kirsty was grateful.

'You're one of the good ones,' she said softly, and he gave her a quizzical look.

'But not good enough,' he concluded. 'I'm fairly intelligent. Don't go fooling yourself, Kirsty. That devil has got you, hook, line and sinker. How he's managing not to come over here and punch my face, I don't know.'

'He'll not do that,' Kirsty muttered, dropping her head. 'He—he's a very sophisticated man.'

'I know,' Guy grunted irritably. 'His civilised habits are a bit thin at the moment, however, by the look of him. If his face gets any tighter it will crack. If he were not such a *sophisticated* man, he would have smashed up every table in the place by now.'

It didn't help much to hear things like that, and Kirsty knew that her hands were trembling. It was even difficult to hold the menu, and in the end Guy took it from her with an exaggerated sigh and ordered for her. If he hadn't been so easy to get on with, and so comfortable to be with, she knew she would simply have run out of the place.

The last time she had seen Adam they had been almost making love, and she had not recovered in any way. She had simply imagined that she had, but the moment she had seen him her stomach had clenched painfully, making her feel sick inside. Without ever speaking he had a hold on her that she could not shake off, and her great fear was that she didn't want to shake it off.

Guy talked to her firmly, making her reply, and gradually she settled down, but her mind was not on anything but Adam. She was halfway through a meal she had not tasted at all before she even began to feel safe. He was just going to go when the business lunch ended. He would not come over to speak to her. She said it firmly in her head and quite convinced herself, so that when Guy looked up and leaned over to take her hand she was stunned.

'They're going,' he murmured, his eyes on her face. 'Now, get your act together fast. He's coming over here.'

The butterflies in her stomach went crazy, and she had about two seconds to stiffen herself up before she found Adam standing by her side, looking down at her, ignoring Guy.

'So, you've deserted the ship,' he surmised in an icy voice, and Kirsty made herself look up at him coolly.

'If you're talking about Parbury Hall, then, no, I'm still there. I'm a working girl, don't forget. I'll be back there tonight.' She looked at him with as fearless an expression as she could muster and knew that unless she attacked, he would. 'How was Portugal? You don't seem to have picked up a tan. Or did you get sidetracked on the way?'

'Oh, I went to Portugal,' he murmured, and she was uneasy at the gleam that came into his eyes as he stared down at her. 'I have to go back tomorrow. Business called me home.' His eyes held hers unwaveringly. 'I know I'm interrupting your lunch, but before I go away again I just had to find out if you had given any thought to the last time we met.'

Kirsty's face went pale, her eyes widened in distress, and she could see the satisfaction on his face as he finished, 'You mentioned that I needed more pictures for my place. Look out for some, will you? Money's no object.'

'I have three already,' Kirsty bit out, angered by the way he had just wound her up so deliberately. He had phrased it like that with one purpose in mind, to fling her back to his lovemaking. If he thought she had been pining away then she would just have to show him that she had not. 'I have a couple of landscapes and a very modern canvas. You can collect them from the gallery any time you like. They'll cost you dearly!'

'You've already cost me dearly, Kirsty,' he murmured. To her astonishment he tossed some keys to the table. 'Hang them for me and charge extra.'

'I'll never go to——!' Kirsty began, but he looked down at her derisively.

'I'll be out of the country by four o'clock today. You have a free hand.'

His taunting attitude did more than anything to set Kirsty's mind right, and she glared up at him.

'How long do I get in safety?' she asked sharply. 'If I'm doing it, I want the place to myself, and, yes, I'll certainly charge you for every single minute of my time.'

'I'm away for a week,' he assured her, and she knew where he would spend most of that time. If she agreed, she would be working in his flat while he spent his time in some hotel with Selina.

'Then I'll do it while you're away—in Paris,' she said acidly. His face instantly darkened like thunder, but before he could speak she threw the final punch, glancing across at Guy. 'You can come with me and help, Guy,' she suggested pleasantly.

Guy didn't have the chance to agree, because Adam turned cold eyes on him at once. 'Don't!' he advised with menacing quiet. 'I've been known to attack innocent intruders. If you don't want to be savagely mauled, keep out of this!'

He stalked out before Guy could react, and Kirsty felt rather ashamed that she had let him in for that ferocious onslaught.

'I'm sorry,' she said in a shaken voice. 'I just wanted to get the better of him. I should never have brought you into it.'

'That's all right,' Guy muttered angrily. 'He only came over here to nettle you. I'm surprised at my *own* sophistication. I could have knocked him flat.'

Kirsty felt like a mouse caught between two larger animals, although she doubted anyone's ability to knock Adam flat. He was six feet two to Guy's five feet eight, and Adam was like toughened steel. In spite of Guy's stocky build, he was no match at all for Adam. She had felt the power of those arms and she was very glad that this confrontation had taken place in a public setting.

When she got back to the gallery she just couldn't settle, and long before they closed she left for home. She knew she did not dare go to Adam's apartment. She had the keys in her bag and the pictures in the boot of the car but going to the apartment was out of the question, and she doubted very much if she would ever have the courage.

When she got home, her father was back early too, and he looked so tired that Kirsty was worried.

'You must be overworking,' she remonstrated anxiously. 'I've never seen you look tired until the other evening, when you were still at it at midnight.'

'I've always worked like that,' he grumbled. 'I can't think what's wrong these days.'

Kirsty persuaded him to go to bed immediately after dinner, but she worried about him all night. He had insisted that he was not ill and yet he looked quite drawn suddenly. Could he possibly have found out about Selina and Adam? She was not at all sure that he would tell her if he discovered anything. It would be just like him to keep it to himself and she could hardly question him on the subject.

If Mrs Drew had been at all normal she could probably have shed some light on the situation. She would have known if her father had been like this before. Mrs Drew was not normal, though, and with nobody to turn to Kirsty had to keep it to herself and worry alone.

By the next day he was much better, and after a weekend of resting he looked pretty much like his old self. At any rate, he insisted on going into the office, and Kirsty set off for work as soon as he had left.

She never got there. On the way she made a decision, and without allowing herself to think over the dangers of the situation she found herself stopping in front of the building that housed Adam's apartment. Very soon she was speeding up in the lift, the paintings with her.

She could not allow him to think that she was scared or that she was hurt about the last time she had been here. She would treat this as a job, another commission, and she would leave as she had come—quietly and without emotion. He would see that it meant nothing to her at all. She would also leave him a large bill!

The silence of the place was at first unnerving, but she walked about for a long time and had a good look around. Her original thoughts did not change. It was stark, lonely, as if he had gone to ground here, as if he didn't care where he lived. The ambience began to seep into her and she knew that she had either to act or go. She couldn't go. Foolish it might be, but she couldn't bear to think that Adam would come back to this place.

Kirsty blanked out emotions and started, and once started she couldn't stop. It would take longer than she had thought, and before lunchtime she was out of the place and setting off to order just what she knew it needed, giving no consideration whatsoever to the fact that she was overstepping the rules. She was supposed to be hanging pictures, but just doing that would somehow make the place worse, like putting bright make-up on a frozen face.

It took a lot of cash but she just kept on, neglecting her own work to do it. In her mind she heard Adam's softly spoken query, 'Are you going to make it beautiful for me?' She *was* making it beautiful, and as the place changed she became more and more excited. She even missed a sale because she was too absorbed in her task to leave it.

Doing his bedroom was tricky. That really was intruding, but it was as cheerless as the rest of the place and she couldn't ignore it. She worked there too, and tried not to think of Adam sleeping in this room, and as the week drew to a close she had finished.

Kirsty took one last look round and felt nothing but pleasure. Everything was rearranged. The huge picture windows were skilfully draped, and that in itself softened the room. There were bright cushions on the white settees and she had searched other galleries daily for paintings to brighten the rooms. She had placed mirrors in strategic places and three huge plants stood in the corners.

Just before she left, she brought her *pièce de résistance* from the car: a very large, straight vase that she filled with brilliantly coloured lilies and placed on the coffee-table she had bought to match the other tables in the room. It added elegance, and she felt smug. She nibbled at her lip about the bill. It had taken a lot of money to do the rooms, and he had not really asked her to do all this, only when he had been trying to soften her up.

That thought annoyed her, and she put the bill on the coffee-table for him to find. It should make his eyes water. She grinned to herself as she left. He had said a week, but if he came back late the lilies would be dead. That was his problem. She went back to the gallery and tried to make up for lost time.

CHAPTER SIX

ADAM came before they closed. Susan was just going home as he came into the gallery and Kirsty was in her flat, gathering the clothes she would need for the next few days. It was difficult being in two places at once and she constantly had the problem of bringing clothes back to her flat and taking things to the hall.

'A visitor,' Susan called up. 'I'll see you tomorrow, Kirsty.' She just heard Susan say, 'She's up in her flat,' and then the door closed.

Kirsty had assumed that it was Karen, who sometimes popped in for a coffee and a chat, but as she heard very masculine steps on the stairs she dropped what she was doing and went to see who had arrived.

Adam was already up the stairs and in the living-room, and for a second Kirsty felt a great flood of alarm. All she could think about was the size of that bill, and his misdemeanours never entered her head at that moment. She just stared at him anxiously and he looked back unswervingly, saying nothing.

'I'm going,' she managed at last, and he nodded, still without speaking.

'Er—what was it?' she continued, and he reached forward, dropping a cheque on the table, the amount a little horrifying, too worrying to speak of, in fact. Kirsty just dared not take a close look, and no thought about where he had been came into her mind. Her own faults were occupying her to the exclusion of anything else at that moment, because she had done almost everything at his flat without permission. And it was not as if she was close to Adam any more; he had left the restaurant in a rage the last time she had seen him.

'It's a lot,' she ventured uneasily, and he began to smile, a slow, warm smile, the sort of smile she hadn't seen for years.

'You made it beautiful. The cost is immaterial. It was almost too beautiful to leave, but I thought I might just catch you before you went home.' He looked at her seriously. 'Thank you, Kirsty.'

'I enjoyed doing it,' Kirsty murmured, feeling very thankful that he was not enraged by her unauthorised actions. 'I might even take that sort of thing up—expand into it,' she added, with an attempt at bravado.

'I hope not. I want to go on thinking that you did it just for me.' He smiled into her eyes. 'I even considered staying there tonight. I could still pick up traces of your perfume as I walked in. The whole thing was astonishing. I never expected it.'

'Did you get to Paris?' Kirsty asked quickly, worried by his dark voice, and he walked forward slowly, until he was looking down at her.

'I got *back* to Portugal. It's where I was heading, if you recall.'

'I wasn't really listening.' She turned away but he caught her shoulder, spinning her to face him.

'So you never actually stopped worshipping, even though the idol fell?' he enquired softly, and Kirsty looked quickly away, managing a slight laugh.

'Don't fool yourself. The work in the apartment was a job, and you've just paid for it. I got quite carried away. I didn't start with the intention of going so far. It simply grew on me. Sorry if I spent too much.'

He ignored her brisk words.

'A lot of care went into it and only you put it there. You did it for me, Kirsty.'

'You've got a wild imagination,' Kirsty muttered, but he tilted her chin and made her face him.

'I've got a long memory,' he corrected quietly, and Kirsty snatched her face away, pulling free.

'So have I! Maybe I was a little sorry for you, but you don't really need any sort of pity. You don't deserve any, either.'

'I couldn't be angry with you at this moment, whatever you said,' Adam murmured. 'One day, however, you'll laugh about Selina. One day, you'll beg me not to speak of her.'

'Don't hold your breath!' Kirsty snapped, looking up at him furiously, her own faults forgotten as soon as Selina's name was mentioned. He could lull her into just about anything. He only had to be there and the past just faded away. 'I'll never find anything to laugh at as far as she's concerned, and as to "one day", there won't be a "one day". I'm only in contact with you now because I had to go back home and you happened to be there!'

She just got that smile again.

'Time will tell. I know a lot more now than I did before.' He turned to leave. 'I'll see you at home. Tell the cuddly Mrs Drew that I'll be there for dinner.'

'But you can't... Why? You know that I can't...'

'Oh, I could stay in my beautiful apartment and keep breathing in your perfume until it fades away,' he agreed smoothly, 'but I'm going to the hall. And, why?' he asked, looking at her levelly. 'Because I've managed without what I need for a very long time. Now I'm not willing to manage any longer.'

He walked out, leaving Kirsty shaken and puzzled. What did he mean? What was he planning? Was it some plot he had worked out with Selina? Whatever he said, she knew he had been to Paris. She paced about thinking, getting more agitated by the minute. It was odd that Selina had neither come back nor been in touch. She had been gone a long time now. Were things coming to a head?

She thought of her father and how strained he had looked lately, his fit of tiredness. He couldn't take any sort of upset, any shock. To find out about Adam and Selina would be too much to bear. It might even kill him!

She had to be there before Adam. If anything happened she had to be right on the spot, to fend off any blow. She threw her things into her case and flew down the stairs, leaving the huge cheque exactly where he had placed it. The only urgent thing, the only important thing, was to get to her father and stand in front of him to protect him.

Impatience made the journey seem much longer than usual, but Kirsty turned in at the gates by the lodge just as Adam was unloading his car, so she couldn't have been many minutes behind him. She was completely worked up inside by now, the terrible thought of what must be coming firmly fixed in her mind like a scene from a film, and, without much thought of consequences, she pulled in behind Adam's Mercedes and got out, rushing round to him.

'Just be careful what you say to my father,' she warned sharply before he could speak. 'While you've been away I've been worried about him, and if you're going to tell him about you and Selina, it can wait. It's waited for long enough, as it is. He doesn't need any sort of upset.'

Her voice was raised and she was glaring at him, and Adam's pleasantly surprised look as she had approached changed to thunderous annoyance.

'I told you that one day I would either kill or cure you, Kirsty!' he rasped, lunging at her and taking her fiercely by the shoulders. 'Right at this moment the killing part is uppermost in my mind. Come into the lodge, because I'm going to put you across my knee and pound some sense into you. I should have done it years ago!'

He looked absolutely furious, and he even made a move to march her in there, but Kirsty dug her heels into the ground and struggled madly.

'Listen to me!' she shouted at the top of her voice. 'I'm not judging you right at this moment. Do what you damned well like. I'm just warning you that my father is not as well as he's pretending to be, and if you cause any trouble, I'll never forgive you.'

'And that's nothing new,' he ground out, glaring down at her, his chest heaving with annoyance. He let her go and looked at her through narrowed eyes. 'What's wrong with Donald?'

'I don't know,' Kirsty confessed, rubbing at the bruised feeling his biting fingers had left on her shoulder. 'I'm just worried. You can have a look at him yourself, now that you're here. He won't have a doctor but I know something is wrong.'

'All right.' He took a deep breath, as if he was fighting the urge to savage her. 'I'll be up there pretty soon.' He frowned down at her blackly. 'If you want things to be smooth and normal, try behaving normally yourself. I know it will be difficult,' he continued nastily, 'you haven't used your brains since you were fifteen, but just this once try thinking instead of reacting wildly.'

'I'm never wild,' Kirsty stated in a starchy voice, and he went back to unloading his car, glancing at her sceptically.

'How useful to be able to cut out the things you don't want to be reminded of. Now, me, I can't do that. Things stick in my mind.' His eyes swept over her, lingering down her figure, and Kirsty felt colour racing under her skin. 'You're wild, Kirsty. If I had a selective memory, that's the bit I would select, but don't let me influence you.'

It was enough to have her hurrying back to her car, and as she drove past him Adam stood watching with a very satisfied smile on his face. It didn't matter that he had won that one, she assured herself. All that mattered was a nice, calm time for her father. He would be delighted to see Adam, and if she had to be charming then she would. Adam wasn't the only one who could be deceitful when the need arose.

The anxiety had been all for nothing, Kirsty decided frustratedly as she got ready for bed later. Adam had been pleasantly polite. He had gone out of his way to treat her like an old friend and it had irritated her beyond words. Even when her father wasn't actually looking at them Adam had been smiling and pleasant, more than pleasant—charming.

Her father had been relaxed and happy, delighted, as she had known he would be, to have Adam back. And, curiously enough, Adam had not said one single word about her work at his apartment. In fact, he had behaved as if he had never been away, and wherever else he had been he had most certainly been to Portugal, because he had hammered out the details with her father over dinner until she could have screamed with boredom.

Kirsty almost threw herself into bed and thumped her pillow in vexation. He had always got the better of her, always got his own way, and now, in some curious and mysterious manner, he seemed to have a grip on her that he had not even had when she was a child. She went to sleep muttering angrily to herself, and she was in no better mood the next day.

Staying in all day was out of the question. It was Saturday and Adam had stated last night that he had no intention of going anywhere. When she went down to breakfast he was even there then, and she looked at him with as much annoyance as she dared. Her father was there too, and she had not forgotten that he must not be upset.

'I'm going into the gallery,' she announced, adding before her father's disappointed expression could grow, 'I really must. Lately I've been neglecting things, and I ought to put in a few hours extra.'

'We'll try to manage without you,' her father said with a smile. 'Back for dinner, darling?'

'I don't know,' Kirsty muttered, avoiding Adam's eyes. When she had said she had been neglecting things he had looked much too pleased with himself, because he knew she had spent the time at his apartment. 'I'll probably have dinner with Guy. Don't make any arrangements for me.'

That disposed of Adam's smile swiftly, and she set off later feeling that she had put him in his place for once. It didn't give her much satisfaction, though, because she didn't really want to go to the gallery and she didn't really want to have dinner with Guy.

All she wanted to do was stay at the hall, watch her father and look at Adam when he wasn't looking at her. She snorted angrily as she drove along. There was no future in that sort of thing, and no honour either. She had known for years what Adam was, but suddenly she didn't want it to be true. No amount of wishing would alter the facts, however, and she drove to her own place and worked furiously, not even bothering with lunch.

And she couldn't face dinner with Guy either. She rang her father and told him she would be late and then she made herself a light meal at her flat and continued working, irritated that Adam was forcing her out of her own home just as Selina had forced her out so long ago.

The telephone rang much later, just as she was about to leave for home, and for a second Kirsty debated whether or not to ignore it. By now she was tired, and in any case she had just locked up her flat. It was not in her nature to walk off blithely and ignore anything, however, and she went back to pick up the receiver.

'Kirsty?' It was Adam's voice, with no derision, no coldness, just his voice as she remembered it from the past, and she knew that something must be wrong.

'Yes.' Without any further words from him, Kirsty felt afraid. He would not be ringing her here if it were not important, and even before he spoke again she knew deep down that it was her father.

'Donald is in hospital,' he told her carefully. 'There's no need to panic. I was there and I acted at once. I'm at the hospital now and I think you should come here straight away.'

'Is—is it the local...?' She couldn't seem to make her lips work. All she could think of was that she had wilfully stayed away all afternoon and evening, just to avoid Adam, and while she had been away her father had been taken ill.

'It's the local hospital,' he said steadily. 'Do you want me to fetch you, or will you manage by yourself?'

'I'll manage. Stay with him, please.' She stared at the phone blindly, the panic that Adam had forbidden rising to the top. 'Adam!' She sounded so distressed that he spoke to her sharply.

'Calm down! He's all right for now. Come here slowly and carefully. You hear me, Kirsty?'

'Yes,' she whispered, and put the phone down, unable to say anything else. It put everything into perspective. Nothing mattered except this. Selina's cruelty to her in the past was suddenly unimportant, Adam's relationship with Selina merely a deep sadness. Now that her father was ill, Adam was there as he had always been, a comfort, a refuge, and it was his steady voice that stuck in her mind as she drove home and turned to the hospital.

He saw her as soon as she came into the lights of the main entrance. This was a small hospital, not the sort of place where people became lost. Everyone knew everyone else here, and Adam was sitting waiting in the narrow corridor. He stood and came towards her as she came in.

'Is it his heart?' Kirsty hurried to him, and he took her cold hands in both of his.

'I thought so, but then I may be totally wrong. The doctor is with him now. They've done a lot of tests. Don't imagine the worst. When they know anything, they'll tell us.'

Kirsty nodded numbly and sat down, and Adam went to the coffee-machine and brought back a hot drink, putting it into her hands.

'It's hot, whatever else it is,' he told her wryly. 'I know you need it.'

Kirsty grimaced and looked down at the steaming liquid, not really bothered how it tasted. 'My antidote,' she murmured. 'You remembered.'

'I remember everything about you,' he said quietly. 'There are too many years to be forgotten easily.' He glanced at his watch and changed the subject. 'We should know something pretty soon.'

'What happened?' Kirsty gave a long sigh and rested her head back, closing her eyes. She felt very tired, almost worn out, and this was the final blow after all the trauma of the past weeks. And there were too many years to be cast aside and forgotten. She had thought she could simply wipe them from her mind but it was not possible. They lingered, and the more she saw of Adam, the more real the past became.

'After dinner, Donald felt ill. He didn't say anything, but it was obvious. When I spoke to him about it he simply said that he was tired, and then he more or less keeled over. I got him here as fast as I could.'

'Maybe I should have done that when he was so tired before,' Kirsty murmured miserably, and his hand came to cover hers.

'No reproaching yourself, Kirsty,' he commanded. 'If he hadn't collapsed, I would have believed him too. You can't insist that someone is ill when they steadfastly deny it. This time is going to be difficult enough without any sort of guilt eating at you.'

It was perfectly true, of course, and Kirsty felt a wave of warmth towards Adam. It mixed itself up with all her other feelings, and when his hand stayed over hers she didn't try to deny him the right. In any case, if he walked out and left her now she didn't know what she would do. She had always needed him.

The doctor came towards them, and as they stood to face him Adam's arm came round her waist, supporting, possessive, and Kirsty just knew it was right, because that was how he had always been until she had pushed him out of her life. He had always been there for her and here he was now, her strength.

'It is not his heart,' the doctor stated firmly, his eyes on Kirsty's pale face. 'At the moment we're not sure what it is, although it could simply be tiredness, as he says. I've been coaxing his work schedule out of him and it seems to be pretty hectic.'

'It is,' Adam agreed grimly. 'There's no stopping him.'

'This has stopped him,' the doctor assured them. 'The body is a wonderful machine. If we don't listen to it, it belts us. We'll continue with the tests, of course, and see what else comes up, but at the moment rest in bed is the best thing for him, and as he's here he doesn't have much alternative.'

'Suppose——' Kirsty began anxiously, and the doctor looked at her very firmly.

'Before he leaves here we'll know exactly what's wrong, and in the meantime we keep an eye on him.' His practised eye moved over her pale face. 'I would say that you need a good night's rest yourself.'

'She'll get it,' Adam said flatly. 'Can we see him?'

'For a few minutes only. We're still busy with him, but I expect he'd like to see his daughter.'

The doctor left and Kirsty went with Adam to a near by room, where her father was lying in a very stiff-looking hospital bed. The sight of him shocked her. He looked pale and weak, and guilt came flooding over her that she had stayed away from home for all these years. If anything happened to him now she would have wasted all that time, just because she had been too hurt to fight for her right to be close to him.

He was really too tired to speak much, but she was able to stand by the bed and hold on to his hand, and just before they left her father looked up at Adam.

'Take care of her,' he said gruffly, and then smiled ruefully at some hidden thought. 'What am I saying? You've always taken care of her. You made a better job of it than I did.'

He sounded very sad, and Kirsty made a protesting noise and leaned forward to him, but the nurse came back and asked them to leave.

'Ring in the morning,' she said in a more kindly way when she saw Kirsty's pale face. 'We'll be with him all night.' And there was nothing to do but let Adam lead her out into the night air of the car park.

'Do you think——?' Kirsty began tremulously, turning to him as soon as they were outside, and his hands came firmly to her shoulders as he looked down at her.

'I don't waste my time speculating about anything. I trust my instincts. You heard what the doctor said. Donald is in the best place, whatever is wrong. We now know he has no heart problems. My instincts, therefore, tell me to stop worrying; they also tell me to get you back home and into bed.'

Kirsty nodded and turned to her car, but he caught her arm and turned her back.

'Right behind me all the way,' he ordered. 'I'll be watching you.'

It brought a smile to her face and she nodded her agreement. 'Thank you,' she whispered, and his dark brows rose sceptically.

'For what? As Donald said, I've taken care of you for years—until you slipped from my grasp. It's easy enough to pick up the reins again.'

He went to his car with no further words and Kirsty got into her own car, her face thoughtful. He had picked up the reins easily, and she had turned to him with the same ease. He was Adam. He was there. He comforted her, caught her if she fell, stood between her and danger of any sort, and now he was here again, as if nothing had ever separated them.

In many ways she had made a success of her life, but always there had been the sense of loss. It had remained even though she had forced it out of her mind. Just for a minute, it wasn't there any more, because Adam had scooped her up into his own life.

At this moment it seemed that Selina was the outsider, had never even existed. But she did exist. She would have to be told about this. Her husband was ill, and the knowledge of that relationship brought Kirsty back to the bitter present. Selina had first claim on her father. She also had first claim on Adam.

He swung out of the car park and Kirsty moved behind him, following as ordered, but now she felt bereft. Adam had not belonged to her since she was a child. It had been a moment of longing, wishful thinking, nothing more. She would follow him if he drove the car off the edge of the world, but he didn't belong to her.

He drove straight up to the house and showed every intention of coming in. It suited Kirsty because she had something to ask him, something to discuss, and it was better to get it over right away. He was not going to be pleased but she could not see any way out of it.

Mrs Drew appeared as they entered the hall and asked how Mr Sinclair was. It was only natural, but there was something about her stance that intimidated Kirsty in her present mood, and it was Adam who answered.

'They're keeping him in hospital, Mrs Drew. We'll let you know when anything happens.'

'He'll need some extra things, then, sir,' Mrs Drew pointed out. 'I'll see to it right away.'

'No! I'll see to it,' Kirsty interrupted in annoyance. Left to herself, the woman would have ignored her, and now she was stepping in to take over immediately. 'Anything he needs will go to the hospital tomorrow. In the morning I'll deal with it myself.'

'As you wish.' Mrs Drew merely glanced at her and left the room, and Kirsty opened her mouth to say more but Adam's hand came round her arm, warning her to stop.

'Not tonight, Kirsty,' he cautioned quietly. 'If you're going to have a stand-up fight with that woman, do it when you're not tired.'

He was right, of course, and Kirsty walked into the small sitting-room, where the remains of a fire still burned brightly. She was probably going to have a stand-up fight with Adam, but he didn't know it yet. She could have done with leaving that too, but it was not possible. She had to take some sort of action. It seemed to be her duty.

'We'll have to let Selina know,' she stated, without looking at him. 'She's his wife, whatever else she is.'

'As you're perfectly correct on both counts, I'll not comment,' Adam agreed stiffly.

At the mention of Selina there was immediate tension, but Kirsty could not just let the matter rest. Her father would expect her to act. He would expect Selina to come back and be at the hospital. She had been his wife for a long time and it was her place to be there.

'Then I'll need to know where she's staying in Paris,' Kirsty said. She took a deep breath and turned to face him. 'I need her phone number there. If you can write it down for me, I'll deal with the whole thing.'

Adam was just closing the door behind them and he stopped quite still, looking at her icily.

'And how do you imagine I can come forth with that information?' The grey eyes had gone as cold as the sea, but Kirsty had to hold her ground.

'I'm not judging you, as I said the other day.' She sighed wearily. 'I just need the information.'

'And, of course, I'm supposed to have it,' he rasped. 'Oh, I can quite see that you're not judging me, Kirsty. What the hell do you think I do? Race across to Paris each evening and get back here for dinner?'

'I know you're not there regularly,' Kirsty snapped, irritated with herself for the hurt she always felt about this, 'but I also know that you've been there, side-tracking from Portugal at the very least. There's no need for this to become unpleasant. Just give me the number, or, failing that, ring her for me. It's something that has to be done. I can't just let it go.'

Adam strode forward and took her face tightly between hard hands, glaring down at her.

'I do not know where Selina is!' he ground out savagely. 'For all I know, she's back in London!'

'Is she?' Kirsty ignored every instinct of self-preservation and looked up at him firmly. 'If she is, then——'

'I said I don't know!' he grated violently. 'Oh, you're really something, aren't you, Kirsty? You fall into my arms and burst into flame. You turn to me when you need comfort or support and yet you have not one bit of trust in me. Donald is more than my partner, he's my friend, and you knew that years ago but you conveniently cast it from your mind. Selina is his wife. She has nothing to do with me!'

'She rang you at your flat,' Kirsty accused him with growing bitterness. 'She was asking you to go to Paris and that's where you've been.'

'Think whatever you like,' he snapped, letting her go and turning to the door. 'Your body grew up but your mind stayed firmly in the past. It hasn't advanced since you were seventeen. Making love to you would have been a tragedy. At least Selina saved me from that. In my saner moments I should be grateful to her.'

'How can I get in touch with her?' Kirsty insisted raggedly, ignoring everything else, but he simply continued to the door, not even glancing round at her.

'Try asking your father. She married him years ago!' he snarled, going out and slamming the door.

From caring about her, comforting her and shielding her, he had now dismissed her, and Kirsty knew she was at least partly to blame. He must have heard the bitterness, the jealousy, and she had to admit to herself that the jealousy had been there for years, eating away at her, making her life empty.

It seemed to have been his final word on any subject, because from then on Kirsty was left severely alone. If she had imagined that with her father in hospital Adam would take care of her, she was mistaken. He never even called at the house, and every time she went to visit at the hospital it was to discover that Adam had been there earlier.

At least they could not find anything wrong. Her father's heart was sound, and even though he was by now restless and anxious to be out, he was persuaded to stay for further tests and the much-needed rest. A slightly high blood pressure convinced him of the necessity and Kirsty was glad to take him books and newspapers, very grateful that Adam had flatly refused to bring any work from the office.

She brought up the subject of Selina with some misgiving.

'We should let her know that you're in hospital,' Kirsty pointed out to her father one afternoon when he was much better.

'I don't see why,' he commented. 'It's nothing serious. Let her be, Kirsty.'

'But she's been away for ages,' Kirsty protested, and he made a wry face.

'That's nothing new. Taking into account skiing, holidays in the sun and buying sprees to Paris, I would say that Selina is away more than she's here. Considering, too, that her boutiques are in London, I don't see very much of her at all.'

Kirsty was stunned. It was something she had not even considered, and her mind went immediately to Adam. He had a flat in London. He went on trips all over the place. Was that how they had managed all these years, without arousing suspicion?

'You're alone a lot,' she said worriedly. 'I'm sorry. I had no idea.'

'You've got your own life to live,' he said soothingly. 'In any case, I'm not exactly alone, there's Mrs Drew.' When Kirsty made a wry face he laughed, and then added, 'Just joking. Actually, there's Adam.'

'Adam? What do you mean?'

'You know what I mean,' Donald Sinclair said. 'Adam is as much at Parbury Hall as he ever was.' He gave her a penetrating look. 'Well, perhaps not as much as when you were there, but even so, he tends to haunt the place.'

It gave Kirsty a lot to think about and she drove away later in a very thoughtful mood. Did Adam love the place so much that he couldn't keep away? Was that what he had meant when he had said that the magic had slipped

through his fingers? And what about his relationship
with Selina? He was enraged every time it was mentioned. He must find it hard to juggle his affection for
her father and still be ensnared by Selina.

Kirsty shook her head and drove on. It was an impossible tangle—too many lies, too much pain. It would
be better when this was all over, but deep down she was
beginning to think that it would never be over. Adam's
hold on her had not lessened. It had grown. There was
a lot more between them now than there had ever been
and it was more compelling than any childhood
adoration.

She made the mistake of calling back at the hall for
something she had forgotten and had a brush with Mrs
Drew that she could well have done without.

'Mrs Sinclair should be informed about Mr Sinclair's
illness,' the woman stated, planting herself in front of
Kirsty as she went back towards the front door on her
way out again. 'She has every right to know.'

'And what makes you think she has not been told?'
Kirsty asked coldly, annoyed at the housekeeper's
bullying attitude.

'She would have been back by now,' Mrs Drew stated
smugly. She folded her hands in front of her and looked
extremely pleased with herself, and Kirsty felt quite
murderous.

'According to my father, she spends a good deal of
time away,' she snapped. 'If I had known that I would
have been here a long time ago and we could have dis-
pensed with your services. If you're so anxious that Mrs
Sinclair be informed, then I suggest you inform her
yourself!'

'I have no idea where she is,' Mrs Drew said huffily,
and Kirsty glared at her.

'Then she can't really think much of you, can she?' she asked icily. 'And, unfortunately, that puts you into the same category as the rest of us. Nobody knows where she is, so I advise you just to get on with your duties and hope she comes back quickly, while you're still employed here!'

She drove off filled with annoyance, because she was quite sure that the woman knew something. She looked exactly the sort of person tht Selina would boast to and confide in. People like Selina always needed a foil for their ego.

Well, Mrs Drew had the house to herself for now, and if she rang Paris, so much the better. Selina would come back and this would all be over. Adam would take up where he had left off, if he ever had left off, and she could get back to the gallery and her own safe little flat.

CHAPTER SEVEN

KIRSTY went to the gallery, grateful that all this was hers. She had built her own security. If it were not for her father she would never have to see either Adam or Selina again for the rest of her life. She would live in an entirely different world. She had tried to do that for years, but her contact with her father had always been a reminder of the past.

Now the past had caught up with her, and she could not shrug Adam off as scornfully as she had thought. Too many things about him reminded her of the way she had felt long ago, and sometimes she seemed to be willingly walking into the very misery that had driven her away.

She helped Susan until closing time and then went up to her flat. It looked neglected. The plants needed water, there was dust on the shining surfaces and she felt a burst of angry energy. Who was she fooling? When this was all over she would be back here with nothing changed. Her life would go on as it had done before, and so would Adam's.

There was no returning permanently to Parbury Hall. She had given that up a long time ago with good reason. This was her place. She had made it all herself, built her life herself, and she had better make sure that it stayed in good order because she belonged here.

She put on some old clothes and began to clean the whole flat, eating her meal standing in the kitchen and then continuing. Gradually, the bitterness faded away, and she worked on with no thought in her head but the necessity to make things look good, her mind seeing no further than the next thing she had to clean. Time passed without her even thinking about it.

It was late when Kirsty set off back to the hall, and when she went down to get into her car the rain had just started. Normally, at this hour, she would have given up the idea and stayed where she was, but she was too worried about her father. The local hospital was not more than three miles from Parbury Hall, and while he was in there, she must be close by.

Before she had gone many miles the fast drizzle had turned into a downpour, and the going was slow on the shining wet road. It was a particularly black night. Headlights dazzled her and the wipers had great difficulty in keeping the windscreen clear. As if that had not been bad enough, as she turned off the motorway her car began to make suspicious noises, and once or twice the headlights dimmed worryingly.

This was something that had never happened to her before. The car might be small but it had always been reliable, and Kirsty glanced anxiously at her watch. It was well after eleven, not a soul about, except for the occasional passing motorist, and if she broke down, she would be very wary of asking for help in this day and age. All she could hope for was that the car would judder on until she reached home.

It was quite lonely out here, not a house in sight, no lights, no people, and by the time Kirsty recognised familiar places in the dimming headlights, the car was just about ready to grind to a halt. Miraculously it kept going, and as the gates of Parbury Hall came into view, Kirsty breathed an audible sigh of relief. She had made it!

Not quite. As she turned in between the gates the car gave a noisy shudder and stopped, every light dying. No amount of coaxing would persuade it to start and she knew without much mechanical knowledge that every electrical part of the car had given up the struggle.

For a moment she sat there, not at all anxious to step out into the downpour, which seemed to have grown worse as she had driven closer to home. One second out there and she would be soaked to the skin. The rain was drumming on the roof of the car and bouncing several inches upwards. As a rainstorm, it really was spectacular, and she even considered sitting it out until the whole thing stopped.

The realisation of the car's position put that thought out of her mind. It was pitch-black, and she was sitting in a vehicle that had stopped right in the middle of the entrance. If for any reason someone should drive through the gates they would crash into her. Sometimes the milk was delivered before it was light, and though that was hours away she couldn't be responsible for the consequences.

As soon as she got out of the car she was drenched, and she knew perfectly well what she had to do. The nearest help was the lodge, and she could only hope that Adam was there now and had not stayed at his flat. He probably had, because there was no real reason for him to be here. Her father was not at home and, as to her, he had apparently dropped her out of his life after their last argument. As he was the only likely help to hand, though, she had to find out.

It was even difficult to find the lodge in the blackness. She had no torch and no umbrella and, as Adam had said, she was not prepared for anything. She stumbled on the path, and only made it to the door because she could faintly see lights behind the closed curtains. At least he was there, and the relief she felt at that far outweighed her anxiety about asking for help.

Once again she was hammering at the door, just as she had been the last time she called here, and once again she felt the need to shout his name at the top of her voice. Rain was running down her neck, her hair was plastered to her head and the discomfort robbed her of her inner qualms about Adam. She needed him! Why didn't he answer?

Kirsty nearly fell inside when the door was wrenched open and Adam stood there, staring at her in astonishment.

'Good God!' He grasped her arm and pulled her out of the pouring rain into the warmth of the room. 'What happened to you?'

He just stared at her, and he seemed to be inspecting her for injuries instead of taking some action, and Kirsty was frustrated with no good cause.

'I broke down,' she said agitatedly. 'I made it this far but now I'm stuck. I'm wet through,' she added unnecessarily, looking down to where the water was actually running off her and on to the floor.

'I worked that out for myself. You'd better get out of those wet clothes right away or, if you feel uneasy about doing that, I'll drive you up to the hall as you are.'

'It's not quite that simple,' Kirsty explained frustratedly. 'I broke down right in between the gates. The car is a danger in that position. You'll have to do something about it.'

She stood there shivering, and Adam stared at her in disbelief for a second. Then he took a deep, indignant breath, eyeing her even more coldly.

'You are the most irritating female I have ever met!' he informed her caustically. 'Why is it that whenever you're in trouble *I* have to be there? How does Wentworth get himself out of these dilemmas? I expect you've been with him all evening. It would have been better if you'd both made a night of it.'

'I have not spent the evening with Guy,' Kirsty protested hotly, furious that he was letting her stand there so cold and uncomfortable. 'For your information, I've been at my flat all the evening, and I've been there alone. I was cleaning the place through, not that it's any of your business. If you don't want to help me, I'll walk up to the house and call the breakdown truck from the village.'

'They'll really love that,' he growled angrily. 'Pouring with rain and almost midnight. It's just the sort of thing they hope for.' He closed the door with a bang and pointed to the fire that was still blazing away in the hearth. 'Stand there and I'll get you something to put on. Don't drip on the rug and say no further words, in case I become greatly enraged.'

'I'll stay here,' Kirsty insisted stiffly. 'Although it would be more humane if you offered me the use of your bathroom. I know this place isn't primitive. It's years since anyone had to wash at a pump in the yard!'

'How remiss of me.' His lips quirked and he looked a little less angry. 'Use the bathroom, by all means, Miss Sinclair, and you can find yourself something to put on. Meanwhile, I'll get my torch and inspect the damage to your car. With a bit of luck, I'll live through this latest encounter with you.' His gaze ran over her and he shook his head in exasperation. 'You're hopeless. Get yourself warm and dry, otherwise I can see you being in hospital next to Donald.'

With that, he ignored her, and Kirsty watched as he searched for a torch and then took an oilskin from a hook behind the door. It annoyed her enormously that he always had the right things to hand. He even had gumboots, and his lips twisted wryly when he looked up as he was putting them on and found her watching him with angry eyes.

'Don't wait for a further invitation,' he murmured tauntingly. 'I'm sure you'll find the bathroom in this small place and you'd better be quick about it, because if I get soaked I'll be dragging you out to take over the hot shower myself.'

Kirsty just glared at him, and he went out and slammed the door behind him, but not before a blast of rain-laden wind had surged in and made the mat by the door even more wet. He had no difficulty in making her feel incompetent. Before she had met him again she had always felt brisk and businesslike. Now she seemed to be always needing him, and he was not slow to point out that fact.

She went in search of the bathroom and had a quick peep into the other rooms *en route*. The modernisation of the lodge had been done a long time ago, when she was still at the hall, but it looked a lot better now. There was the main room that led directly to the outside, a small modern kitchen, one bedroom and a bathroom with shower. It was certainly not a place for anyone with a family, and she had often wondered how people had managed to live in such places in the past.

The furniture must be Adam's, because this place had never been furnished, and Kirsty wondered if Selina had helped him put up the curtains. That brought her back from her musing, and she instantly felt grim about things. How often had Selina been here with Adam, not a mile from her husband's home?

She pushed the thought from her mind, and the hot shower warmed her chilled skin as she stepped into it. After drying herself, Kirsty put on the white bathrobe she had found hanging behind the bathroom door. It was obviously Adam's, because it came down to her ankles and she had to tie it tightly round her and turn up the sleeves. It was warm, though, and covered her completely. Everything she had been wearing was soaking wet, and there was no chance of drying it out over any radiator.

In the kitchen she found a plastic bag and pushed her clothes into it, and then she had nothing to do but wait for Adam to come back in. She couldn't see any sign of him when she peered through the curtains. It was still lashing with rain and black as pitch outside. He would be very wet by now, and in no good mood either.

Curiously enough, she wasn't too bothered about that. It was cosy in the lodge and she put more logs on the fire and then wandered back into the warm bathroom and tidied up after her shower. Adam's things were in there, his talc and aftershave, and she couldn't resist taking the top off the bottle and smelling it. He had always used the same sort and the scent of it brought back memories from a long time ago.

She even remembered the first time she had noticed it, when they had been down by the river on a hot summer's day. It was probably the first time she had thought of Adam as anything other than her dearest friend and she had wanted to lean across to him and put her face close to his skin. Even now the scent of it was slightly erotic, and Kirsty quickly put the top on and placed it back on the glass shelf.

Her face was a little flushed at her thoughts and she hurried into the living-room quite guiltily, going over to stand uneasily by the fire, as if she had been doing something sinful. The thoughts wouldn't go away either, and the early memories of her teenage yearning for Adam mixed with the memory of being with him in his flat, the exciting feeling of his hands on her.

A shiver of pleasure ran over her skin and her face felt even more hot. That was when the door opened and Adam came back, and she could see that he was very wet, even with his oilskin on. His black hair was as plastered to his head as her own hair had been and, when he had rid himself of the wet oilskin and gumboots, he turned his attention to Kirsty.

'You do need the garage for the car. It's beyond me,' he told her with a brief, irritated glance in her direction. 'I've moved it, however. I towed it on to the grass.'

'You had to get your car and a tow-rope?' Kirsty asked anxiously, quite seeing that she had put him to more trouble than she had really intended.

'I wasn't exactly up to towing it by hand,' he muttered, casting another irascible glance in her direction. 'Obviously it will have to stay where it is until morning, then one of us will have to phone the garage. I expect it will be me.'

'I can do that,' Kirsty said quickly, worried by his continuing irritation. 'You don't have to do everything for me.'

'What a relief,' he taunted acidly. 'I was thinking of giving up my job to take care of you.'

'I'll make some tea,' Kirsty offered uneasily, a little anxious about the way his eyes glanced at her rather disdainfully. It looked as if he was not going to stop being annoyed and she was in a very awkward situation, with no transport and no clothes.

'A brilliant idea,' he murmured testily, 'but I warn
you, if you scald yourself, you're on your own. My good
deed for the day is over.'

He disappeared in the direction of the bathroom and
Kirsty nibbled at her lip and went to the kitchen. She
hadn't expected him to be so annoyed. He had always
taken her problems in his stride. Normally he would have
got over any irritation by now, and she still had to ask
him to take her to the hall. She had to borrow this robe
too. It made her take extra care with the tea-making.

Kirsty had just brought the tea in when Adam came
back, showered and changed into dark jeans and sweater.
There was a two-seater settee in the room and he dropped
down to that, taking the hot drink she handed him with
a nod of thanks but not a single word. His continuing
attitude made her more apprehensive than ever, and she
sat on the very edge of the facing chair and glanced at
him worriedly.

He was gradually making her unsure of herself, and
she realised that only too well. Since they had met again
he had been cruel, mocking and scornful. On the other
hand, he had made love to her, had been kind to her
and taken care of her, both when she had had the
migraine and when her father had been taken to hospital. Now he was ignoring her. He had become a very
complicated character and she couldn't cope with it.

'I'll have to go home,' she blurted out when he just
sat there and drank his tea, his eyes on the flames that
darted up from the logs.

'Later.'

Apparently that was all he intended to say and Kirsty
felt a wave of dismay. Any later and it would be the next
day, but she couldn't very well order him to get up and

take her to the hall. She chewed at her lip, trying to think
of something to say that would calm him down.

'Is the furniture yours?' she finally asked, and he
glanced at her without any interest.

'It was in my flat before I had the whole place altered.
Some of the stuff I gave away, the rest I brought here.'

'It's nice,' Kirsty offered nervously, glancing round
the firelit room. The light was reflecting the shine on
very good wood, and it must have looked quite elegant
in his flat. Some great turmoil must have made him throw
things out and change to the rather barren style he had
created before she had intervened.

She glanced up at him, wondering why he had done
that, and he was watching her intently, the firelight
making his eyes look incredibly clear. It threw her into
a greater state of agitation and she looked away quickly,
putting her drink down on the near by table.

'Who made the curtains?' she asked hurriedly, wanting
to keep things as soothing as possible.

'Why?' His brief question stopped her in her tracks,
and she looked at him uneasily.

'No reason. I—I just wondered. I—I was thinking
about the difficulty of putting them up and...'

'I had them made,' he volunteered wryly. 'A woman
in the village.'

'Did she put them up?'

'No.' He put his cup down and went on looking at her
in that watchful, mocking manner, and Kirsty found
herself saying something she had never intended to
mention.

'I expect Selina helped to put them up.' She was hor-
rified when the words came out. She had seemed to have
no control over them. The thought had been in her head,
and with it a feeling of near desolation. It was cosy in

here, homely. She could have curled up all night here with Adam, watching the fire, talking as they used to talk, but always the thought of Selina intruded, and the words had come tumbling out.

Adam just looked at her steadily, no expression on his face, and Kirsty felt colour rushing up under her skin. He had turned out on a night like this to help her. She was even wearing his bathrobe, and still she pried into the relationship that ate at her thoughts always.

'I'm sorry,' she gulped. 'I can't seem to help saying things.'

When she dared to look up at him again he was still watching her, but now his eyes were narrowed, speculative, a slight smile edging his lips.

'Come here, Kirsty,' he ordered softly.

Of course she didn't mean to move, but he just went on looking at her, his eyes holding hers almost hypnotically, and she ran her tongue round suddenly dry lips, her whole expression apprehensive.

'Don't, Adam,' she begged in a shaken voice, but he ignored her plea and went on looking at her.

'Come here,' he commanded in the same soft, dark voice, and Kirsty found herself getting to her feet and moving towards him, her eyes held by his. She seemed to be doing it in a trance, unable to keep away from him, and as she came close he reached forward and caught her hand, pulling her down to him, cradling her on his lap, bringing her head to his shoulder when she murmured anxiously and made a move to get up.

'I—I should go home,' she protested, but she knew it was all because of her nervous excitement. She was close to him and everything else seemed to be unimportant, not even remembered. There was even the same scent to his skin, like some beautiful, warm memory of long ago.

'You are home.' He tilted her head back and his glance slowly moved over her face. 'I've never seen you look quite so much at home in all the years I've known you.'

Kirsty closed her eyes, desperate to escape from the smoky grey temptation of the eyes that held her as securely as his arms. Her heart was racing already, threatening to leave her body. Memory mixed with feelings. The last time she had been held so close had been at his flat. She had never recovered from the erotic force of that. It lured her on, making her still and submissive.

What sort of person was she that she could be here like this when she knew all about him? He was becoming like a drug she needed. Her whole body was waiting with a breathless desperation, and yet she knew all about Selina. She had always known. He held Selina like this too.

'No!' She moaned the word piteously, tears forcing their way beneath her dark lashes, and his hand curled round her face, holding it up to the light.

'Yes,' he said, quietly implacable. 'Wherever I am, that's where you belong, because you're mine. You always have been, and I won't wait for you any longer. I can't.'

Kirsty opened her eyes, the clear green depths shimmering with tears.

'You're going to—to force me to——?' she began in a heartbroken voice, and his smile grew to sensual amusement as he stroked back her hair.

'I've never hurt you in your life, angel-face,' he reminded her softly.

'You have! And not only me, either. There's my father to consider. What will he do when he finds out about Selina?'

She had held a forlorn hope that the mention of Selina would enrage him, make him release her and take her home, but he just went on looking at her, the smile edging his lips, and she knew that she didn't want to go home. In spite of everything, nothing could have made her move from him.

'Right now, you're not thinking of your father. You're thinking of yourself and me. You're unhappy because you're jealous, and it's such a sad waste of emotion.' His face came closer and his lips brushed hers. It was electric. Such a small caress had waves of excitement shivering through her. She was aware that she was cradled on his knee, that his arms were tightly around her, that the fire crackled comfortably in the grate and that the room was silent and warm. 'There is no Selina,' he breathed into her mouth. 'There's just the two of us and everything we want.'

'You don't know what I want,' Kirsty cried frantically, although her head was thrown back in a wanton manner, inviting his lips to the silken skin of her throat, and he accepted her invitation, his mouth nuzzling against her, finding the opening of the robe and searching her skin urgently.

'I do know what you want,' he breathed raggedly. 'You want me. You're here with me, softly warm and just a little desperate. I'm aching for you and you're going to belong to me.' His mouth came back to hers, his tongue circling her trembling lips. 'Aren't you, Kirsty?' he demanded, and she gave a shuddering cry, her hands reaching for him, her mouth opening beneath his.

'Yes!' she whispered, and his lips crushed hers as his hands slid into her robe and took possession of her breasts. At the same time his mouth opened over hers and consumed her.

Kirsty cried out against his mouth, and he lifted his head and began to kiss her face fiercely.

'Whatever happens,' he murmured unevenly, between heated caresses, 'you're mine tonight, Kirsty. The phone can ring, the river can overflow and the world can stop turning, but nothing will make me let you go.'

His desire was too urgent to allow him simply to kiss her face and neck. He lowered her down to the soft cushions of the settee and parted the robe, his eyes following the movement of his hands as he stroked the whole of her body. Beneath the robe she was completely naked, pearly-tinted in the firelight, and nothing was hidden from his gaze, but Kirsty was too committed to feel embarrassment.

It was all right to be with Adam, to feel his hands on her, to allow him to touch every secret part of her. Her hands reached out for him of their own volition and her fingers tore at his sweater, whimpers of frustration escaping from her lips each time his mouth moved from hers to taste another part of her.

He obeyed her small, demanding cries and pulled the sweater over his head, dropping it on the floor, and he did not need to guide her hands to his body. She reached out with a shuddering sigh of pleasure and ran her fingers over the hard expanse of his chest and shoulders, teasing him until he growled low in his throat and took her hands in his, his tongue moving erotically over each palm.

'Let me touch you,' she gasped, struggling to free herself from his exquisite torture, and he brought her hands down between them, guiding her to the place she would never have dared to seek alone.

'Then really touch me,' he ordered raggedly. 'Don't tease me when I'm burning up inside.'

She ran her hands over him, excitement flaring more hotly as he twisted in frustration and crushed her lips with his.

'Do you know how long I've waited for this?' he asked against her mouth. 'Do you know how I've dreamed of it, wanted it? You've made me wait a long time, Kirsty.' He ran his hands hotly over her body, his breathing uneven and pained. 'I've waited years to own you.'

'Adam!' She moved her hands to his shoulders, her fingers digging into his skin, and he looked down at her fiercely, his eyes dark with passion.

'Does Wentworth touch you like this?' he demanded hoarsely. 'Does he?'

'No! Never!' She looked up at him with wide, dazed eyes. 'I wouldn't let anyone...'

'I'd kill him!' he growled through clenched teeth. 'If anyone ever touched you but me...!'

He looked so fierce, so possessive, that Kirsty felt a wave of unease as he stared down into her face, his glance moving slowly and possessively over her hot cheeks.

'You look seventeen again,' he said more quietly. 'How could I have even imagined that you would let anyone else close to you? Jealousy is a very painful thing, isn't it, angel-face?'

His hand moved, stroking her, and Kirsty tossed her head wildly, feeling she would die if he moved away from her.

'I lost you!' she cried helplessly, tears springing to her eyes, and he leaned forward, kissing her eyes closed.

'You didn't,' he assured her softly. 'I've wanted you since you were seventeen. It's just taken a long time, but now we've arrived.'

He lifted her easily, holding her tightly against him, and she knew where they were going. Her whole mind was given up to Adam. Nothing else mattered except the driving painful need to belong to him.

In the lamplit bedroom he slid her robe away, and placed her on the soft bed before undressing and joining her there, and Kirsty felt the whole of his body against hers for the first time. Strangely, it was something she had never imagined, and as she felt the strength of him against her she went wild in his arms, winding herself round him, touching him frantically and placing heated kisses on his face and shoulders.

He restrained her, his breathing raw in his throat as he forced her to lie beneath him as he slowly kissed every part of her.

'Not yet,' he ordered softly as she whimpered in frustration. 'Drive me on like that and you'll be hurt.' She went still. It was something she had not thought about and he caressed her slowly, looking down at her, seeing the momentary fear in her eyes. 'Relax, Kirsty,' he breathed. 'Relax, sweetheart.'

His tongue moved over her breasts and a wave of voluptuous pleasure swept over her, her body moving sensuously against him as warmth flooded through every part of her. Kirsty gave an excited cry as her fingers clenched in his hair. His erotic enjoyment added to her excitement, and she pulled him closer, cradling him against her.

'Oh, please don't stop!' she gasped, and she heard his low laugh against her skin as his lips moved lower, following his stroking hands as he aroused every part of her to fever-pitch.

Kirsty began to sink into a world of sensation that took all thoughts from her head but delight. She tossed beneath him, consumed with pleasure, and she was so lost that the cry that rose from her lips as he entered her strongly was a wild cry of pain mixed with rapture.

He was still at once, his lips covering hers, and as she dared to relax again he looked down into her eyes, his own eyes burning with triumph.

'You're mine, Kirsty,' he told her fiercely. 'At last you're mine.' He kissed her gently, his hand stroking her hair. 'Now I'm going to love you,' he said softly. 'Now I'm going to show you what pleasure is all about.'

He began to move, his breathing uneven and harsh as he felt the honeyed warmth that surrounded him, and Kirsty's shocked enjoyment turned to disbelief at the feelings that flooded through her. Without any conscious thought her body moved with his and she wound her legs round him, forcing herself closer, fusing them together.

Waves of electric excitement coursed through her and the wild cries she heard were hardly recognisable as her own. Her fingers tightened on his shoulders, her nails digging into his skin as the power of Adam's body forced her into a matching rhythm.

She had known him for most of her life, but there was a primitive urgency about him now that thrilled her and changed him into another being. His drive to possess her was so pleasurable that for a few seconds she thought she would not be able to bear the excitement, and then, just as she thought that this was the greatest wonder of her life, her body went into spasms of fulfilment that shattered her world into blinding light and swirling velvet.

She could feel Adam's arms around her as he too fragmented into ecstasy. His lips were against her skin, murmuring encouragement and pleasure, reassuring her and holding her with him in a wildly spinning world.

'Kirsty! Sweetheart,' he gasped. 'My angel. You're beautiful.'

She heard him but she was floating on clouds of sensual contentment, her body too tired to move. It would have been impossible to speak, and when Adam collapsed against her for a second she was drowsily lifeless.

He rolled away from her and gathered her close, but he had to lift her into his arms, and she turned towards him with no thought but to stay as close as possible.

'Adam.' She whispered his name sleepily, and his hand stroked down her body before he drew the sheets over both of them.

'I know,' he said softly. 'Go to sleep now, Kirsty. I'll be here.'

Her head came to his shoulder, and the last thought she had was one of delight that she could feel his body against her own. It had always been Adam. All her life it seemed he had been there, adapting to her needs, caring for her and asking for nothing. It seemed so right that what she had finally given him was herself.

CHAPTER EIGHT

WHEN Kirsty awoke it was already daylight, the morning sunlight seeping in through the closed curtains of the room, and for a second she was disorientated. Then she remembered. She had been here all night, slept with Adam's arms around her, her body curled intimately with his.

The full implication of what had happened hit her then. She had let him make love to her. She had been overwhelmed by the same urgency herself, had been demanding and wild in his arms. The feeling of shame was almost unbearable and she could not bring herself to blame Adam alone. He was a man and such things meant nothing to him. He was thirty-five, almost thirty-six, and probably had more than one woman even though there was Selina.

No, she had to take responsibility for her own actions. She had been eager to belong to him, fiercely glad to have him back. Facing him now was something else again, though. Facing her own image was difficult enough, but the thought of Adam's grey smoky gaze made her reluctant to leave the warmth of the bed.

She could hear him moving about in the kitchen and she knew she would have to go in there and brave it out as soon as possible. She slid out of bed, embarrassed now by her nakedness, colour rushing into her face when she remembered last night. Adam had ensnared her masterfully. She had been no match for his determination to possess her. She had had no defence against his expertise, against the sensual pleasure of his touch. Even now feelings washed over her in great waves as she thought about it, but in the light of day she also knew her own shame.

There was still nothing to wear but the robe, and she found it folded on a chair. He must have put it there as he got up, and she wondered what he had been thinking then. Had he looked at her with triumph or scorn? She didn't even know if she had been well wrapped up. Kirsty tied the white robe around her and steeled herself to face him. She was afraid because she didn't know how he would be. He might expect that this would just continue, or he might look at her with cool amusement.

The kitchen was close to the bedroom in this small place but she managed to slip into the bathroom without encountering him, and she only felt safe behind the locked door. In the mirror, a pale face looked back at her. Her hair was tousled from sleep, and from the way Adam had threaded his fingers through it last night, her eyes were heavy, and it seemed that another person was staring at her. One night with Adam and she was defenceless, hopelessly vulnerable.

She made the best of things, straightening her hair with her fingers, washing her face in cold water and trying to rub some colour into her pale cheeks. Her bag was still in the other room, she thought, in fact she couldn't even remember whether or not it was still in the car. She didn't even have a lip-gloss to hide behind, but she couldn't stay there all day. Kirsty took one anxious look at herself and then opened the door.

As she walked into the kitchen, Adam turned from the cooker and glanced at her, his eyes narrowing as he saw her face.

'Sit at the table,' he said quietly. 'Breakfast coming up right now.'

'I don't want anything,' Kirsty told him almost in a whisper. 'I—I'm sick.'

He turned fully round to look at her, his eyes running over her pale cheeks, seeing the way her lips trembled. Her eyes were shadowed, almost desperate, and one swift glance told him that her hands were trembling even more than her lips. She looked so helpless, so young, that for a moment his own lips tightened in anger, a picture of how she had been at seventeen flashing unwillingly into his mind.

'Tea!' At this brusque order, he pushed her firmly to a chair, and seconds later placed a steaming mug of tea in her hands. 'Drink it, Kirsty!'

She tried, but her teeth had a tendency to chatter against the cup and her hands trembled so much that she had to put it down. She was much too aware of Adam's lean height as he stood close by and the hot drink was no antidote now.

He watched her steadily, and then turned off the cooker where he had been preparing breakfast for both of them. When she still sat with bowed head, he strode over and pulled her to her feet, making her look at him.

'All right,' he said forcefully, 'talk to me!'

'I want to go home.' Her face flushed slightly at the words that sounded so childish in her ears, and she tried to correct the impression. 'Last night . . . I don't know why I let it happen. I must have been mad to let you . . .'

'Seduce you?' he enquired coolly. 'Is that what you're telling yourself now, Kirsty? I seduced you and you're sorry it happened?'

'What do you expect me to be but sorry?' she countered sharply, looking up at him with enormous green eyes, grasping at anger to cover her feeling of shame. 'I know I was partly to blame. I just let you lure me and—and all the time I knew perfectly well that I was just somebody who happened to be there.'

Inside, she knew she was trying to goad him into retaliation, trying to make him so annoyed that her embarrassment would go. Instead of angry he became very quiet, he let her go and looked at her levelly, his face showing no emotion whatsoever.

'So you happened to be there,' he agreed calmly. 'Let's follow that through, shall we? You arrived wet and bedraggled, changed into my bathrobe, and I was so overcome with lust that I ravaged you.'

'I never said that!' Kirsty's head shot up, and she stared at him in near horror. 'What I'm saying is that I was vulnerable and——'

'And I took advantage of you,' he finished for her swiftly. He put his head on one side and regarded her steadily. 'Right. I agree with that assessment. So, to conclude, I took advantage of you, you slept with me, and now you're sorry.'

'Ashamed,' Kirsty whispered, dropping her head.

'You *enjoyed* it, angel-face,' he reminded her quietly. 'I had to restrain you more than once. You were all woman and you never screamed for mercy. Face it, because it's the sort of thing that's more or less final. The virginal room is inappropriate from now on.'

Kirsty turned away, colour flaring in her cheeks.

'How do you know that I wasn't already...? There was no way you could tell, and...'

When she looked round he was smiling in a provocatively reminiscent way, his eyes half closed.

'Don't say that to me, Kirsty,' he insisted softly. 'I can still feel you beneath me. I can still feel the softness of your skin. It's a tempting memory.'

'I want to go home,' she whispered, panic at the back of her voice, and he shrugged indifferently.

'OK. I'll drive you up there. I've already called the local garage. Maybe they can repair your car by lunchtime. If they can't, there's always Donald's car, or Selina's.'

She knew he had said the last name with deliberate cruelty, and Kirsty suppressed the cry of pain that came to her lips and made for the door, expecting him to follow. She had to get away from here very fast. She needed to be alone to think things out.

It was only as she got to the door that she realised she had no shoes. Her own were somewhere in the kitchen, with the plastic bag of wet clothes. She had to turn again but he was right behind her, amused at her predicament, the bag and her shoes in his hand, her handbag under his arm.

And the shoes were still damp when she slid her feet into them. They were uncomfortable and probably ruined. It was almost necessary to hobble to his car and he didn't offer to help. He just dropped the rest of her things at her feet in the car and went round to drive off—an unfeeling taxi-driver who had never seen her before.

The journey seemed much longer than it actually was because Adam simply drove and looked straight ahead, and Kirsty felt tears pricking at her eyes. How could he be like this when only last night he had been making love to her, whispering sensuously in her ear, setting her world on end? She just didn't know him any more. This morning she was not anyone special to him.

'How could you be like this?' she choked as they drew up in front of the house. 'How can you treat me so—so coolly, when last night...?'

'When last night I was enjoying the delights of your body?' he asked almost casually, turning to her as she sat there devastated. 'You've already answered that yourself, Kirsty. I seduced you. You could not have made it plainer. Unless you want me to take you back down to the lodge and seduce you again, I seem to be powerless.'

'Last night I forgot about Selina!' she cried angrily, and he nodded with thoughtful deliberation.

'So did I,' he mused. 'I'll forget about her again, the next time I make love to you.'

'There won't be a next time!' Kirsty said wildly, her eyes widening in panic, and he just looked at her with a taunting smile, his eyes running over her.

'Not until we're alone again,' he agreed. 'But when we are alone, you'll come to me the moment I say your name.'

Kirsty shook her head violently, too scared to speak and deny it because she had the terrible feeling it was true. She had always been deeply ensnared by Adam, even when she was a teenager, and now she was quite lost, and if she didn't belong to him, she didn't even know who she was. The dilemma could only be solved by keeping away from him permanently.

She opened the door to get out, because it was quite clear that Adam meant simply to sit there and continue to goad her. And it was as the cooler air drifted across her leg that she realised just what a spectacle she presented.

'I can't go in like this!' she said in agitation, turning to him for help with no hesitation now she was in a fix.

'Why not?' he taunted softly. 'Tell Mrs Drew you've been for a swim in the river and a passing vagrant stole your clothes.'

She stared at him as if he had gone mad and he looked back blandly, no sign of amusement on his face.

'Please!' she begged frantically. 'The longer I sit here, the more intrigued she'll become.'

'Well, if you don't like my first suggestion,' he mused, 'try telling her to mind her own business. Failing that, you could dance in there and let her know that you're wearing my bathrobe because you slept with me. That should silence her.'

Tears of rage, embarrassment and self-pity stood in Kirsty's eyes as she looked at him angrily, and he reached forward and touched her face gently.

'Ignore her,' he said softly. 'Walk in there and ignore her. She's nothing to you.'

'Will—will you come with me?' Kirsty asked tremulously, and he sat back, shaking his head.

'No. My days of being your saviour, guardian and protector are over. Every time I see you I'm going to want you. Remember that.'

'You're forgetting about Selina,' Kirsty choked, getting out of the car, and he looked at her steadily.

'Not really,' he murmured. 'I seem to be stuck with her. But then, she's away a lot, as you know. That leaves us.'

Kirsty just grabbed her things and ran to the house, and his grey eyes followed her every inch of the way, his expression a mixture of wry amusement and pity. She seemed to be no older now than she had been when she had first looked at him with the glowing green eyes of approaching womanhood and set his pulses racing. A wave of fierce pleasure raged through him, clenching his stomach, tightening his face, and then his eyes narrowed thoughtfully as he turned the car and drove back down the drive, leaving Kirsty to find her own solutions.

Mrs Drew was there, as expected, almost as soon as Kirsty walked through the door, and there was more scorn than intrigue in her eyes.

'I didn't know you were back yet,' she said, making it clear that she had been well aware of Kirsty's absence, her cold eyes taking in the bathrobe, so obviously a man's, and Kirsty's rather wild appearance. It was the sort of scornful look that Kirsty had endured for years from Selina, and it was enough to stiffen her resolve and give her the much-needed courage.

'Only just,' she agreed pleasantly. 'My car broke down in the rainstorm last night and I had to stay at the lodge. Let me know if the garage rings, will you?'

She went up the stairs, well aware that the acid face was now very thoughtful. It would give her something to pass on to Selina. The realisation of that took the slight smile from Kirsty's face, and she hurried to her room without stopping to get rid of the wet clothes. One day soon Selina would be back, but now she couldn't wait around for the event. Seeing Adam again was out of the question. He had stated his intentions very clearly.

There were slight bruises on her skin that were obvious as she stepped under the shower, and as she noticed them the full impact of last night came back. She felt too wrung-out to cry about it, and in any case the thrill was still there, shivering through her when she least expected it. If he spoke her name she would do exactly the same thing again, and that was not going to happen. Never in all her dreams of him had she envisaged that she would become Adam's mistress. As far as she was concerned, he had one already, one who was glossy and hard, a good match for him.

But the problem of going away and leaving her father when he was still not well appeared to be unsolvable, and she found herself almost wishing that Selina would come back home, and leave her with no alternatives at all.

The garage fixed the car and returned it sooner than Kirsty expected and when she went to the hospital it was to find that her father was much better. The doctor came to have a word with her just before she went in.

'We're letting him come home in the morning,' he told her. 'Just see that he takes it easy. I've had a word with his partner earlier today and told him that your father needs another week away from the stress of work. I would think that the two of you together would be able to make him see reason.'

So, once again, Adam had been there before her, and Kirsty nodded and smiled but she knew that there would be no way she could work with Adam, even to protect her father. It left her with even more problems, and she went to the gallery but spent the rest of the day worrying.

When Guy phoned she refused to go out as nicely as she could. That was all over. She was not the same now, and she even thought that people would be able to see it just by looking at her. She could see it herself, every time she glanced in the mirror. In some mysterious way, Adam had left the mark of his ownership on her expression. There was a wistful twist to her mouth, a slight sadness in her eyes. She felt lost, and even if nobody else could see it, Kirsty saw it herself.

Guy was not easily put off. Just before the gallery closed, he appeared. He came in smiling, flowers in his arms, and Kirsty felt a great flood of regret that she could no longer go on meeting this calm, agreeable man. He was patient, kind, a pleasant companion for any woman, but at the side of Adam all other men paled into insignificance. Besides, things were now very different. It would be cheating.

'You sounded depressed,' he said as she greeted him. 'I expect you want to get home, but I thought these might cheer you up.'

'You're kind, Guy.' Kirsty smiled. 'I have to get to the hospital later, to take my father's things in. He's coming home tomorrow. I can make you a coffee, though.'

It pleased him, and Kirsty led the way up to her flat, wondering how she was going to tell him that she could not see him any more. She hated to hurt Guy but it was cruel just to go on when there was no future in it.

She made the coffee and he sat watching her, smiling as she handed him a cup and sat facing him.

'Nice and cosy,' he murmured, glancing at her, and it was an unfortunate remark. Last night she had been thinking how cosy it was at the lodge. It brought everything into her mind and she felt her face tighten with misery.

'Not another migraine?' Guy asked worriedly, and she shook her head, unable to speak for a second. 'Then I hit a raw nerve,' he assessed accurately. 'It's Frazer, isn't it?'

'Yes.' Kirsty hung her head and then glanced up anxiously. 'I can't see you again, Guy. I'm sorry. We've known each other a long time, but there really is no sort of future in it.'

'Because you love him,' he stated quietly, and she just nodded her head. Of course she did. She always had done. There was nobody but Adam, there never had been, and now it was all so much more painful.

'I'm sorry,' she whispered. 'I never meant to hurt you.'

'And is he hurting you, Kirsty?' Guy asked astutely.

'It's unavoidable,' she murmured. 'Some things can't be changed. I've always known that, since I was little more than a girl.'

'Would beating him up help?' Guy asked wryly, and at least it had her smiling.

When he left she left with him, locking the gallery and preparing for the drive to the hall, and they stood for a moment in the street.

'Goodbye is a bit final,' Guy mused. 'Can we leave this as it is for the moment, Kirsty?'

'I'd like to say yes, really I would,' she told him, her hand coming to his arm. 'It would be cheating, though, and I care too much about you.'

'Well, I won't leave the country,' he said with a smile. 'You know where I am. If you need me, or if you change your mind...'

He reached to kiss her cheek, but at the last minute pulled her gently into his arms, kissing her unresisting lips.

'Keep fighting,' he whispered against her hair, and then he turned and got into his car, driving off with a wave of his hand, leaving Kirsty looking after him with regret on her face.

The expression didn't last long. She looked up and Adam was striding towards her, his face white with rage. He looked so angry that she had the momentary inclination to take to her heels and escape from him. He was in front of her, though, before she could take any action, panic-stricken or otherwise.

'So you intend to keep the boyfriend?' he ground out immediately. 'Have you acquainted him with the latest facts?'

'I was just saying goodbye,' she began, defensive at once, but he wouldn't let her continue.

'Obviously!' he snarled. 'I saw you say hello, too. I saw the flowers and the warm greeting when he arrived!'

'You've been watching me? You have no right to spy on me!' Kirsty exclaimed, feeling completely cornered. 'I've been doing exactly as I like for years and my relationship with Guy has nothing to do with you.'

'It would have been, if he'd stayed in that flat for long,' Adam rasped, his hand clamping on her arm as she tried to turn away and escape. 'I'm not much given to sharing. Warn him to stay away from you if you have any friendly thoughts about him. His safety depends on his absence!'

He was so domineering and possessive that Kirsty felt anger rising by the second, and she glared up into his furious face, snatching her arm from his grasp.

'My father is coming out of hospital tomorrow,' she reminded him. 'The moment he's fit to be left I'll be back here and taking up my life again. Guy is part of it. What I do is my affair, and one night isn't going to change that!'

'I'll be here every day,' he grated savagely. 'I'll haunt you!'

'You'll be too occupied with Selina,' Kirsty snapped, looking at him with scornful eyes. 'I've been feeling ashamed of myself because of last night and the way I behaved. How stupid. You should have enough shame for both of us.'

'I've got enough determination for both of us,' he threatened, and she spun away, making for her car.

'Leave me alone!' she snapped. 'I still feel as I've felt for years, disgusted by the sight of you!'

He let her go, although for a moment she thought she had gone too far. She managed to drive away, but she was trembling so much that after a minute she had to pull to the side of the road and try to recover. Why had he been there? He had never said. Did he think that after last night she would be constantly at his beck and call?

And what were his plans for when Selina came back? He was forbidding her to see Guy, even when he knew that Guy was not her lover and never had been. There was no doubt about Adam's relationship with Selina— a long and continuing relationship. It made her feel ill just to think about it.

The next day, Kirsty went by herself to bring her father home. She half expected Adam to be there and she was dreading it. She knew perfectly well that he ought to be at work, but he seemed to have the ability to appear when she least expected to see him, and she was almost looking over her shoulder all the time.

Her father was very glad to see Parbury Hall and to be back home after his enforced stay in hospital, but Kirsty was no longer delighted with her surroundings. Thoughts of Adam were in every room, and in spite of all the things she had said to him there was such a deep unhappiness inside her that she wanted simply to go and not come back.

Admitting to herself and to Guy that she loved Adam had left her even more defenceless, and she thought of Selina with more bitterness than ever. Selina would sail through, whatever the final outcome of this. She had always won, and Kirsty felt no more able to fight for her own rights than she had ever felt. She had never been any sort of match for Selina. In any case, she could not fight for Adam. He didn't love her.

Her own unhappiness made her fuss over her father so much that just before dinner-time he had to speak severely to her.

'I'm not in a wheelchair, Kirsty,' he reminded her sternly. 'One more week and I'll be back at work. Nobody is turning me into an invalid, not even you.'

'I just want to look after you,' Kirsty protested. 'It frightened me when you were ill. Pretty soon I'll be going away again, and I want you to be perfectly fit before then.'

'Why are you going away?' her father asked sombrely. 'This is your home, Kirsty. I want you here. You don't know how much happiness it's given me to have you back.'

'I can't come back.' She sank to the carpet and leaned against his legs. 'I don't fit in when Selina is here. I never have done. I can't fight her now, any more than I ever could.' She looked up anxiously. 'I'm sorry. I shouldn't have said that. She's your wife.'

'Listen, love——' he began urgently, but a voice from the open doorway stopped him as Adam walked in unannounced.

'So you're back, Donald. Can I interrupt this delightful domestic scene?'

Her father beamed at Adam and Kirsty leapt to her feet, almost ready to take flight. Last night she had raged at him, but there was no sign of annoyance on his face. Instead there was a look of quiet determination that was almost as worrying.

'I'll check on dinner,' she said hastily, making for the door, and her father called after her.

'There's something I want to tell you, Kirsty.'

'Later,' she muttered, her eyes avoiding Adam's as she hurried past him.

In her heart she had known he would be here tonight, but that had not helped one bit in allowing her to face him. She would have to be there at dinner too, and she looked down with impatience when she realised that her hands were trembling. She had no idea what her father had been about to tell her but she could well imagine it was some plea for her to live in harmony with her stepmother.

How impossible! With Selina back she would know where Adam was every spare minute that he had. Her only hope was to go back to her own life and try to forget. Not that Selina was hurrying back. If Mrs Drew had telephoned her then Selina must have decided to ignore it—unless she was on her way back now? The thought gave Kirsty more forebodings, and she tackled the housekeeper almost without thought, the desire to be prepared uppermost in her mind.

'Have you heard from my stepmother, Mrs Drew?' she asked outright, when she had informed her that there would be one more for dinner.

'As I told you, Miss Sinclair, I have no idea where she is.' The woman didn't even turn from the cooker, and Kirsty's hands clenched in silent rage. No other household would employ this woman and put up with her attitude. Her father would be completely at her mercy if he was by himself and ill.

She was still angry as she went back to the drawing-room, where her father was listening quietly to Adam. The conversation stopped as Kirsty came into the room and her father noticed her flushed face.

'What's wrong?' he asked sharply, and Kirsty grimaced and then managed a slight laugh.

'Just temper. It will be a good job when I get back to London. Much longer here and I'll either fire that woman or hold her head under the cold tap.'

Adam's lips twitched and her father grinned at her.

'You might just get the chance one day soon——' he began, but Adam glanced at him sharply and once again interrupted, changing the subject entirely. It surprised Kirsty. Adam's manners were usually impeccable, but when she looked at him in wide-eyed astonishment he simply ignored her and went on talking.

All the way through dinner he dominated the conversation too, and as most of it was about work Kirsty soon felt left out. Every time her father spoke to her Adam was ready to break into the conversation and bring up another subject. It made her feel unwelcome, and as soon as she could she made her excuses and went out. She was too worked up inside simply to go to her room, however, and finally she put on a jacket and slipped quietly out of the house, walking in the gardens in the soft light of the moon. She looked round with nostalgia, because before long she would have to leave here, and this time it would be final; her relationship with Adam made that certain.

Kirsty was just going back into the house as the front door opened and Adam came out. He looked as surprised to see her as she was to see him. She had known his car was there but he was leaving much earlier than usual and she had no way of avoiding him.

'I—I thought you would be staying longer,' she managed uneasily, and he just looked down at her in the moonlight.

'And I thought you were in bed. I realise that I bored you out of the room.'

He wasn't being apologetic, and Kirsty looked at him sharply. He was normally an entertaining dinner-time companion and usually she could listen to him all night. It suddenly dawned on her that he had deliberately stopped her father from speaking twice, and had then monopolised the conversation to keep a grip on things.

'I'll get in to my father,' she said quickly, but he shook his head with every appearance of satisfaction.

'I persuaded him to go to bed.'

Kirsty really felt suspicious then, and she faced him again, dreading his answer to the question she knew she must ask. 'He knows, doesn't he? He's found out.'

'He knows,' Adam agreed calmly, 'but it's nothing that worries him. Therefore, it should not worry you.'

'Are we talking about the same thing?' Kirsty questioned sharply. 'Are you telling me that he knows about Selina and you and that he's taking it happily?'

'I think he's secretly delighted,' Adam mused wryly. 'She's quite a liability. He probably feels as if he's stopped banging his head against a wall.'

Oh, Selina would be a liability to anyone, but even if her father had tired of Selina, he loved Adam like a son. Kirsty just stared at him in horror, not knowing at all what to say to this outrageous disclosure, and he suddenly began to laugh. Apparently her expression amused him, and Kirsty's eyes sparkled angrily at his sheer audacity.

She opened her mouth to tell him what she thought but he caught her hand and held it fast.

'Oh, Kirsty,' he laughed. 'You're so naïve. You haven't changed a bit.'

'You mean, I'm a fool?' she cried hotly. 'I agree. I must be to have fallen for your tricks. You don't care about anyone, do you? At least I thought you cared about my father, even though you've stolen his wife.'

'Maybe he just wanted to pass her on,' Adam suggested, still laughing down at her. When she tried to pull free and storm into the house he jerked her towards him and captured her in the prison of his arms.

'You don't understand,' he told her firmly, his laughter dying. 'But whether you're outraged or not, don't bring this subject up with Donald.'

'Because he's devastated by your duplicity!' Kirsty announced fiercely, too angry to be aware that he was holding her.

'Duplicity?' he mused darkly, looking down into her face. 'It depends whether you mean treachery or craftiness. Let's just say that he's surprised, and he doesn't need any more surprises at the moment.' He looked at her intently. 'You see, Selina is coming back tomorrow.'

Even though she had been expecting it almost daily, Kirsty felt bereft at the news. For a while she had been here at Parbury, breathing in the magic of the place, being with her father. For a while too she had been with Adam, and, even though she had known it could never be, she loved him.

'So you got in touch with her!' Kirsty accused him miserably, and he shook his dark head, his glance roaming over her desolate expression.

'No, angel-face,' he said quietly. 'She rang me at the office this afternoon.'

'Then, why didn't she ring my father?' Kirsty whispered, knowing that this proved all she had known for so long, and knowing that it was the very end for her with Adam.

'She rang me because she wants to be quite sure that she has a future.'

Kirsty pulled away and he let her go. She couldn't stand there and listen to him any longer and she went into the house, closing the door and leaning against it for a second. He had shocked her with his matter-of-fact way of dealing with this. Adam was not at all as she had thought him. Underneath that smile, underneath that caring attitude, he was as hard as Selina, and now they had arranged their future.

CHAPTER NINE

WHEN she woke up the next morning, Kirsty's greatest inclination was to escape. She didn't want to be here when Selina came. She didn't actually want to hear it said openly that, from now on, Selina would be with Adam. She could not escape, though, because there was her father to consider. No matter how well he seemed to be taking this, Kirsty knew that he must be grieving that Adam had deceived him. She had to stay and be there, and she would have to keep her own grief hidden.

At breakfast she managed to hold her tongue about the forthcoming events, but her father looked strained and seemed to be struggling even to speak at all. He soon excused himself and walked off to his study, and Kirsty watched him go with a great deal of anxiety. She had always thought of him as a strong man but now he looked older, and more shaken than she had seen him look since her mother died. No matter how well Adam thought her father was dealing with this, Kirsty knew he was suffering, and that alone made her decide to see things through.

She seemed to spend the morning wasting her time, watching the drive for some sign of Selina. Adam would have gone to pick her up, and she knew that sooner or later she would have to face the sight of them both getting out of Adam's car. They would be together, and it would be a picture that would set their future and hers.

When Adam's Mercedes came swiftly up the drive just after lunch, Kirsty wanted to move away from her window and not see them, but she was held there by some miserable force that was like a desire to punish herself. As he got out of the car she bit into her lip painfully, seeing once again how his blue-black hair caught the sunlight, watching the way the light angled the planes of his face. In all probability she would never see him again after today, and she made a small noise of distress when she realised she was imprinting the sight of him on her memory.

Selina was not there, and for a moment Kirsty could not believe it. As Adam walked alone into the house she peered down anxiously, trying to see into the car from this height, wondering if Selina had decided to stay there and leave the discussion to the men. Not only was that unlikely, but there was no one at all with Adam, and Kirsty's mind seemed to be spinning frantically as she tried to solve the problem. Adam had been quite sure that her stepmother would be here today.

She went down to face things, but there was nothing to face. She could hear her father and Adam talking in the study. Adam's voice was very firm, and she waited for arguments but none came. Finally, she just walked in there, knowing her place was beside her father, quite prepared to battle with Adam if it was necessary.

It was her father's expression that surprised her. He looked annoyed that she had just walked in uninvited.

'Give us a minute, Kirsty,' he ordered brusquely, obviously waiting for her to go, but Adam intervened.

'We don't need a minute, we need coffee,' he stated firmly. 'The discussion is over, Donald. Stick to what I've told you and leave the rest to me. It's my field of expertise, after all.'

'More than I can expect you to do——' her father began as Kirsty watched with a puzzled look on her face.

'It's a pleasure,' Adam said grimly. He glanced at Kirsty with the same grim look on his face. 'Get us some coffee, will you?' he asked briskly. 'And don't be too long. We don't want Mrs Drew hovering around. Selina will be here very soon.'

Kirsty just turned and went out, too stunned even to be hurt. What was the matter with her? Was she peculiar? The two men had been calmly planning the future like a business deal, her father handing over his wife to Adam with no animosity—he had even looked grateful. His only bit of annoyance had washed off on her, as if she was too stupid to understand such sophisticated arrangements. He was right, too. She did not understand. Nobody seemed to have any feelings. She had seen more acrimony at sales over the ownership of some picture.

Kirsty didn't even see Mrs Drew. She got the coffee herself and took it back, although she felt more in need of a brandy to sustain her through this coming ordeal. By now she could not even picture the ordeal at all. It was outside her most bizarre imaginings. At this moment she felt that she could not even begin to comprehend the way either Adam or her father thought. An arrangement was being made that left her speechless.

Selina arrived about ten minutes later, and by that time Kirsty's nerves were screaming. The three of them had been sitting in polite silence since she had brought the coffee, and at any moment she had expected either her father or Adam to ask her to leave. They had not, but from time to time she looked up and found Adam watching her sombrely, and it was almost a relief when they heard the sound of a car coming up the drive and stopping outside the door.

Adam strolled to the window and looked out.

'Selina,' he announced, a look of cold satisfaction on his face. 'Now we can sort out our lives at last.'

Kirsty got to her feet, preparing to leave them to their grotesque arrangements, but his voice stopped her in her tracks.

'Where are you going?' His voice was harsh, commanding, and she gazed at him in dismay.

'This has nothing to do with me,' she managed shakily. 'I can't bear——'

'Kirsty, love——' her father intervened, but it was Adam who controlled the situation and his voice held her to the spot.

'You stay, Kirsty!' he ordered sharply. 'Leave this room and I'll come after you. Nothing happens here unless you stay. You hear every word that's spoken.'

Kirsty was stunned by his cruelty. She just stared at him in distress. He was determined that she should listen while he arranged to settle his future with Selina. She turned away blindly.

'I can't!' she choked, but she had not taken two steps before Adam was beside her, his hand on her arm.

'You can,' he insisted quietly. He looked down into her pale face, his eyes suddenly dark, brooding. 'You owe me this, Kirsty.'

When he looked at her like that she couldn't refuse, because whatever he had done, or was about to do, she loved him.

'All right,' she said helplessly, and his hand slid down her arm, his fingers finding hers and curling round them warmly for a second.

'Stay by Donald,' he said softly, 'and keep your nerve. For a few minutes, he might need you.'

Kirsty didn't know how she made her legs take her back towards her father. She could hear Selina's crisp high heels tapping on the parquet floor in the entrance hall, the sound coming closer and closer, every step signalling the end of her own life near to Adam.

And then Selina stepped into the room, as beautiful as ever, her face glossy and well made-up. She made Kirsty feel like a bedraggled girl. She was dressed in a lovely deep blue suit, that brought out the bright blue of her eyes, and not a golden hair was out of place on her well-poised head.

Kirsty looked at her hopelessly. Selina was older than Adam by five years, but she didn't look it. She was at the very peak of her feminine powers and the knowledge of that glowed on her face. Just the sight of her after so long told Kirsty that she had never stood any sort of chance with Adam. She just could not compete.

Her hand went to her father's shoulder and he covered it with his, and she thought it was significant that he did not get up as Selina entered the room. He was too shattered about what was to be said, and her hand tightened comfortingly beneath his. Adam had been right. Her father did need her, not only because he had been in hospital either. He was dreading this, but not as much as she was dreading it herself.

'Surely we're not going to have our discussion in front of everybody?' Selina asked sharply as she stopped in the doorway. Her eyes came angrily to Kirsty and then flashed to Adam. 'What is this, a committee?'

'Deeply interested parties,' Adam assured her. He was unsmiling, watchful, and Kirsty glanced at him quickly, looking for some welcoming sign on his face as he saw Selina. All she could detect was a sort of cold triumph.

'Very well. I suppose she would have to know sooner or later. It doesn't bother me unduly.' Selina walked in and sat down, crossing her elegant legs and then looking at her husband. 'I'm assuming, Donald, that Adam told you I want a divorce?'

'He did.' It was all her father said, and Kirsty's hand tightened even more beneath his, her fingers gripping his shoulder to give him support.

'Well? Do you agree?' Selina asked sharply. 'We don't want this to be messy, do we? You have your business reputation to consider and I'm quite prepared to divorce you quietly and just disappear.'

'You've very considerate, Selina,' Donald Sinclair murmured. 'Adam and I have discussed this and he has all the details.'

For the first time, Selina looked suspicious. She glanced at Adam and then back at her husband.

'Surely your lawyer——?' she began, but Adam interrupted smoothly.

'We'll get around to lawyers in time. For now, though, I would imagine money is uppermost in your mind. As I deal with money, naturally Donald has left things to me.'

Kirsty looked at him in surprise, suddenly unsure again, unable to understand. He did not look as she had expected him to look and the eyes he turned on Selina were coldly grey, not a hint of warm appraisal in them. He was perched on the edge of an antique desk that stood in the room, everything about him relaxed and certain, as if he intended to enjoy every minute of this.

'It's not exactly the right way to go about things,' Selina snapped, her composure definitely rattled. 'This is between Donald and me or, at the most, some solicitor who can act with discretion.'

'Oh, I'm discreet,' Adam assured her silkily. 'As you know, I've been discreet for about ten years. I astonish myself.'

'What you have been for ten years is nothing to do with me,' Selina said sharply, but Kirsty was intrigued to see that, beneath the make-up, her smooth skin had gone rather pale.

'It has everything to do with you, Selina,' Adam corrected. 'But we'll let it pass, as things have worked out at last. You will not divorce Donald. He will divorce you.'

'I refuse!' Selina said heatedly, but Adam smiled at her in a very threatening manner.

'My dear Selina, you have no choice. The grounds are adultery. The proof is in my safe.' She suddenly looked much older, and he took advantage of her silence to press home his point. 'However, Donald is prepared to be generous. He will divorce you on the grounds of incompatibility, or whatever grounds the solicitor thinks best, but there is a catch. You get nothing.'

Selina jumped up and glared at Adam, before turning furiously on her husband. 'Why are you just sitting there, saying nothing?' she demanded shrilly. 'This has nothing to do with him. As to getting nothing, I can claim a very substantial amount.'

'But you won't,' Adam put in coldly. 'If you do, the grounds will be adultery, and neither you nor your boyfriend would want that. You have been—what is that wonderful word?—consorting with an important, married public figure for ten years, to my knowledge. Refuse Donald's generous offer and he will sue for divorce for adultery, and all the details of that affair will come out. Of course, you'll be on television, and that might boost your sales at the boutiques, but, honestly, I don't think the man in question would like it at all.'

'You're damned clever, aren't you?' Selina raged, sinking back to her seat, her face red with chagrin.

'Brilliant!' Adam smiled at her wolfishly. 'I've had you sewn up for years but you just didn't know it. You thought I suspected, Selina. I didn't suspect, I *knew*. All

I had to do was wait for Donald to express his dissatisfaction with you. Then I told him. Before that, it would have hurt him, now he's quite gleeful. You'll notice that if you look closely.'

Kirsty felt almost faint, not as yet able to sort out her own emotions. For years she had blamed Adam for something that was nothing to do with him at all. She watched him now with a look almost of awe. She had accused him, reviled him. Why had he never told her? What would his attitude be towards her now? She still could not face it, because all the beliefs of seven years were falling at her feet.

'So I get nothing?' Selina said dully, looking defeated for the first time in her life. There was none of the scorn on her face that was usually there, and Kirsty stole a fearful glance at Adam when she realised that he had added to Selina's humiliation by insisting that she herself stayed in the room. And she partly understood why. This long-standing affair of Selina's could only have been humiliating to her father, and Adam cared about him. He was a dangerous adversary who protected his loved ones.

'I told you that Donald was prepared to be generous,' Adam assured her silkily. 'You can have the boutiques.'

'Thank you for nothing!' Selina snapped, glaring up at him. 'They're mine already!'

'Not even on paper,' Adam corrected. 'Donald put up the money and I arranged the transactions for him. Knowing the situation even then, I behaved very carefully. All you own, Selina, is the name over the door. You have never repaid a penny of the money that was advanced for the boutiques. It might have seemed that Donald was just reaching into his pocket when you demanded more and more, but actually everything is on paper as loans. Donald even owns the stock, to be perfectly truthful.' He glanced across at Kirsty's pale, bewildered face. 'Now, his daughter, on the other hand, repaid every penny he lent her—to such an extent that I sometimes wondered if she was living on bread and water. Kirsty owns her thriving business. Donald owns yours, Selina.'

'This can't be legal!' Selina raged, after one glance of hatred at Kirsty.

'It is,' Adam stated flatly. 'Of course you can try to fight it, but it would be a waste of time and money and you would lose. You would also get bad publicity. In any case, as I said, Donald is prepared to give the boutiques to you as a settlement, just as he is prepared to find other grounds for divorce, providing you do exactly as you are told.'

'This is blackmail!' Selina cried angrily, and Adam smiled that wolfish smile again.

'Fairly close to it,' he agreed, 'but all perfectly legal. It's called an arrangement. You should understand that. You've had a clandestine arrangement for ten years at least, and this is much more straightforward.'

Selina jumped up and began to storm out of the room, but Adam's voice stopped her, his tone like a steel whip.

'Well?' he bit out. 'We want an answer now!'

'Do I have any choice?' she asked bitterly.

He looked at her with a very bland expression on his face before he said quietly, 'No. You don't. You ran out of luck years ago, soon after you met me, in fact.'

'I underestimated you,' Selina sneered. 'I imagined you just disapproved of what you thought was my occasional fling. In fact, I actually thought you were too wrapped up in Kirsty to notice. Of course, I should have known better. You're a clever, sophisticated man, and there's not much to interest you in a girl like that.'

'Be careful, Selina,' Adam warned softly. 'It would be very easy to talk yourself out of your boutiques.

Donald loves his daughter and I'm not at all generous. The gift of the boutiques is his idea, not mine. Left to me, you would have had your moment on television.'

'I'll pack!' Selina snapped, knowing it was useless to say more. 'I can't wait to get out of here.'

She went out of the room, and for a second Adam's eyes stayed on the doorway, his expression cold as ice. He then turned, and Kirsty could see that he was fighting rage. She had seen him do that before.

'Well, you managed to live through that, Donald,' he said heavily. 'Don't weaken, because she'll struggle to the end.'

'I know.' Her father's hand came up to squeeze Kirsty's. 'Don't worry. I'll not give one inch. I want Kirsty back more than anything in this world.'

Adam looked at her then, his eyes narrowed and steely grey.

'I can't think of one excuse she could come up with for living elsewhere now,' he said coldly. 'Unless, of course, she prefers her flat in London and her interesting life there.'

Kirsty knew he was reminding her of Guy and the things she had said outside her flat, and now she was completely at his mercy, because everything she had thought about him was untrue. She didn't know where to begin with apologies, and by the look of him Adam was in no mood to accept any. He might never be in a mood to accept them either. By not trusting him she had lost her chance to be with him. She had lost it years ago.

'Kirsty, pour us all a drink!' Donald Sinclair said heartily. 'We're acting as if Selina had won. We should be celebrating.'

Kirsty was glad to have something to do. Now that he had made his point, Adam didn't look at her, and even the satisfaction he had obviously felt as he dealt with

Selina seemed to have gone. She turned away to get the drinks, but instead of talking to her father, Adam stood looking out of the window, and there was something so forbidding about him that even her father kept silent.

The scene was changed as Mrs Drew came into the room and looked for once unsure of herself.

'Mrs Sinclair has told me that she's leaving,' she told Donald. She paused uneasily and then finished, 'She wants me to leave with her.'

In other circumstances, Kirsty would have been laughing, but at the moment there wasn't a smile in her and her father had to deal with the situation alone.

'Then leave with her, Mrs Drew,' he advised. 'It seems to be the best thing to me.'

'It will seem like desertion, sir——' the woman began, and Kirsty could see that she was now undecided as to where her own best interests lay. 'You'll have no housekeeper.'

'I have my daughter. I'm quite sure we'll be able to manage until some other person can be appointed. It would be a good idea to pack your things now, Mrs Drew, and leave with my wife. I'll have a cheque ready for you before you go.'

He could not have made it plainer that he wanted her to go and Mrs Drew nodded and left the room. The old order was over and she knew it, and by the look on her face she was totally reassessing the situation.

'Is that all right, Kirsty?' her father asked quietly, and she managed a smile.

'It couldn't be better. We'll start looking for someone tomorrow. I can manage by myself until we get fixed up properly.'

'And you'll stay—live at home?' her father asked with a trace of anxiety.

'I can't see anything stopping me,' Kirsty reassured him. 'I can get to the gallery every day. Maybe I'll turn my flat into another showroom. It means I'll be able to expand for next to nothing.'

She was uncomfortably aware that Adam was both watching and listening, but he didn't attempt to join the conversation. It made her feel that they were cutting him out, and she gave him a quick, despairing look that was met with total inflexibility. He was not about to forgive her. She had accused him wrongly four years ago and had let him know that she had suspected him since she was seventeen. It was a long time, and she could see that it was utterly unforgivable.

'I'll go and start preparations for dinner,' she murmured, quite desperate to get out of the room and away from the atmosphere.

'Let me take you both out to dinner tonight,' Adam suggested, but his voice was cool and Kirsty didn't even look round.

'I like to cook,' she muttered, making her way to the door. 'I don't particularly want to go out. It will be nice to have the kitchen to myself and it will give me something to do.'

She made her escape and hurried towards the kitchen, but Selina was just coming down with her first load of cases, and she stopped as Kirsty looked up at the stairs.

'So, you're back with Daddy!' Selina pronounced nastily. 'I expect you'll fly back into the nest like a dreary little bird. Don't expect things to be as they were when you were seventeen. I was well aware that Adam fancied you, but men are like that, always after the young girls. He's considerably more important now than he was then, and you're not exactly alluring.'

'Just go, Selina!' Kirsty said coldly. 'You've done your damage and there's no one left to damage now. I can be pretty sure that you don't know a thing about Adam. His contempt for you was about ten miles wide, and I seem to remember that he told you to watch your tongue.'

'Why? Will you run and tell that I've been horrid to you?' Selina mocked, and Kirsty summoned up a taunting smile of her own.

'Horrid things haven't happened to me,' she pointed out. 'You were at the receiving end of all that and, as Adam mentioned, I own my business. Yours seems still to be in the lap of the gods.'

She walked into the kitchen as the smile died on Selina's face, but her own smile faded too. Selina could not cause any damage now, but she had already caused it. She had caused it long ago, and even then she would not have been able to do it if Kirsty had trusted her heart.

A few minutes later Adam walked in, and, after one quick glance to see who it was, Kirsty turned quickly back to the sink where she was preparing the potatoes.

'We're going out for a meal,' he announced uncompromisingly. 'Your father wants to celebrate his good fortune.'

'I can cook a meal to celebrate——' Kirsty began, keeping her back turned to him, but he interrupted harshly.

'Donald wants to go out. He feels guilty about you being in here working and he wants to take you out.'

'I never seem to have much alternative, do I?' Kirsty murmured, dropping the knife and standing with bowed head. 'I don't feel like being merry.'

She turned to find him regarding her with steely-eyed concentration. He watched her for a minute and then shrugged.

'I'm just the messenger. Take the matter up with Donald. Invite Wentworth down here to join the party. Maybe that will bring a smile to your face.'

He walked out before she could answer, and Kirsty went to her room and began to get ready. She knew she should be feeling glad. Selina was out of their lives, even Mrs Drew was gone, but the house seemed particularly silent when Adam was no longer part of her life.

Her father seemed to be utterly unaware that there was an atmosphere of gloom. He had thrown off the burden of Selina as if it had never been there, and it made Kirsty more than ever certain that both Adam and her father had known about this for a while. Neither of them had confided in her. She seemed to have been left out, just as she had been for years.

Next day, Adam moved out of the lodge and back to his apartment. Her father grumbled that it meant seeing less of Adam, but at least he would soon be back to work and would see him there. Kirsty felt she would be lucky ever to see Adam again. Of course, she could have apologised immediately, but her crime seemed to be too extreme for mere words of regret. Adam had shown no tendency to bend, and she just did not have the nerve to seek him out and try to set things right.

When her father returned to work Kirsty got back to the gallery, only coming home at night, and, with the advent of two dailies and a very motherly housekeeper, things seemed to be following a pattern for the future. Adam stayed away, and when she asked about him Donald Sinclair said that a lot of work had piled up at the office and there were one or two overseas visits to make.

Two weeks later, Selina walked into the gallery when Kirsty was there alone. There was still that air about her that worried Kirsty, and she said the first thing that came into her head.

'What do you want?'

'Just browsing,' Selina murmured, looking round at the pictures. 'I've never been here before. I wondered just what you had. I may very well buy something.'

'Of course, you'll need to set up a place of your own now that you're not at Parbury Hall,' Kirsty agreed, deciding that nothing would intimidate her. Selina was looking for trouble, but at that moment Kirsty couldn't think of any she could cause.

'True,' Selina mused, looking closely at the displays. 'Of course, I wouldn't normally bother to come right out here, but I know how well you did Adam's apartment and I wondered if you did it professionally or if that was just a special thing for him.'

'It was a favour. I'm glad you were impressed, but I don't do anything but buy and sell pictures,' Kirsty said sharply, disguising her feeling of despair. So, Selina was seeing Adam. Immediately the little devils of doubt came racing into her head. Had all that scene at home been to cover up the future for both of them? Had it been to let her father down lightly? Adam had left the lodge at once and he never came now. Suddenly, nothing had changed, except that this woman was now out of her life at the hall.

'Oh, I haven't seen it,' Selina assured her, turning to smile one of her acid smiles. 'I can't imagine a situation where Adam would even speak to me, let alone invite me to that fabulous place. No, I just heard about it. The woman in his life just can't seem to stop talking about it. She says it's a delightful atmosphere to live in now. Apparently she hated it before you got around to doing it. She might very well come in to see you before long, because she wants some other things and won't hear of anyone but you getting their hands on the décor of the apartment. Adam just lets her have her head, of course. You know how indulgent he can be.'

'No doubt she'll be in touch,' Kirsty muttered. How could she ever have thought that Adam did not have women in his life? In fact, she had mused over that matter before. It was different, though, to realise that someone was actually living with him, sharing the apartment that had been done with such love and care.

Kirsty managed to keep up a front until Selina left. It was all too apparent why she had come. This was a blow she'd felt she had to strike. It was not threatening, it was merely friendly gossip. Even her father could not have found any malice in it. Only Kirsty knew how cruel the visit had been. It had closed the last door between herself and Adam, and it had closed finally.

When Selina left Kirsty put up the closed sign, even though it was only late afternoon. She could not face any customers and she was just glad that Susan was taking a well-earned day off. Up in her flat, she had a good weep and then gathered her things for home. Little by little she was transferring her clothes and private possessions to Parbury, although the joy had gone out of being there. Adam had always made the place magical for her and now he never came.

His visits would be very rare from now on, because he had someone to keep him in London, and even when he did come she knew she would not be able to face him with any show of indifference. It seemed that one thing had led to another, and although with Selina's going her prayers should have been answered, they had not been answered at all. She had finally lost Adam, and she knew that she could not in any way blame him. Her lack of trust had set the scene for the final act. It was not some small quarrel that had got out of hand, she had let him down long, long ago. If making love to her had been his way of punishing her for the past, then how could she blame him?

CHAPTER TEN

A FEW days later Guy called at the gallery, again as Kirsty was preparing to leave for home, and when she looked at him a little reproachfully he simply grinned at her and began to walk around, viewing the pictures.

'I'm buying,' he assured her. 'Or, at the very least, I'm ordering.'

'You don't have to, Guy,' Kirsty said softly. 'I told you how things were because I want to be scrupulously fair. It doesn't mean that I'll shriek and faint if I see you.'

'I know,' he laughed. 'Honestly, though, it's not just my desire to pester you. There's a move in the boardroom to beautify the place. Being too cautious to buy expensive works of art that might increase in value even more, the idea is to collect for next to nothing and accumulate over the long-term.'

'The very long-term,' Kirsty pointed out, amused by this logic from such high-flyers. 'What did you have in mind?'

'Believe it or not, I have a free hand,' Guy informed her wryly. 'That being the case, it's friends first, and as you constantly spring into my mind I'm here to ask for advice.'

'I can collect for you,' Kirsty mused thoughtfully. 'If you go to other galleries and get them to do the same it should be possible to gather a few pictures together that will grow in value.'

'Talk it over at dinner?' Guy asked eagerly, and she looked at him long and hard and then nodded. Why not? She had been very open with him, and he knew exactly how she felt about Adam. But Adam was out of her life and it was pointless simply to wallow in the pain of it.

'All right,' she agreed. 'Not tonight, though. Early next week. Have a plan worked out. I'll want to know exactly how much you're prepared to spend and exactly what you'll expect for it.'

'You'll also want to know that it's not a trick to sneak back into your life,' Guy said drily, and she nodded, giving him a bright smile.

'That too,' she agreed. 'It's Friday. By Monday you should be able to come up with some idea of what you want.'

Guy stayed around for a while, keeping the conversation strictly on business, quite clearly interested in everything she had to say. They didn't leave the showroom, and as she locked up and prepared to leave for home Guy walked out with her, but this time he simply waved goodbye and drove off. It left Kirsty with a warm feeling, and the knowledge that she was important to at least one member of the opposite sex, not despised, as Adam probably despised her.

And thinking of him seemed to conjure him up, because when she walked to her car she felt a wave of shock to see the long, dark lines of a Mercedes parked on the other side of the road. The man who leaned against the bonnet and watched her unswervingly slowly straightened up as she saw him.

Adam! It was weeks since she had seen him, and for a moment Kirsty thought she was hallucinating. He was real enough, though, and he was intent on confronting her. She realised that as he came forward, and stood waiting for a break in the traffic so that he could cross the road.

What did he want? Was he coming to make another scene about Guy being in the gallery? Was he coming to inform her that he had a woman permanently in his life? There was nothing at all he could say to her that she wanted to hear, because anything he said would only make the hurt worse.

Kirsty almost fell into her car, scraping her key about, desperately trying to get it into the ignition. She gave him one anxious glance, and the fact that she was about to drive off had not escaped his notice. He was standing on the edge of the pavement opposite, unable as yet to cross to her, but his face said more than any words, and as she looked at him she saw him call her name impatiently. She slammed the car into gear and shot off as soon as a small gap in the traffic allowed, and she had no time to see whether or not he had gone back to his car to follow her.

Even if he had, she told herself, there would be a long delay before he could pull out and then find a place to turn. She could be well away before then. All the same, he would catch her on the motorway, if catching her was his intention. Her own car was no match for the Mercedes, and she knew Adam's driving skill. She veered off on to the old road. It was heavy with traffic but she never normally used that road and he would not think that she would use it now.

Half an hour later, and after many hold-ups, she came to the place where the motorway ended and the road to Parbury began. From here she had no choice, but by now Adam would have given up the chase, thinking, no doubt, that she had gone somewhere else. Kirsty slowed and signalled, joining the traffic coming off the motorway, and as she settled for the remaining drive she felt safe. No confrontation with Adam, no recriminations. In all probability he would not try to see her again.

Adam's car slid smoothly in behind her. Kirsty saw him as she glanced in the mirror and she knew she had not fooled him at all. He had simply taken the motorway and pulled off to wait at the junction when he had not overtaken her. Now he was right behind her, and she wouldn't even be able to get into the house without encountering him. By now, she didn't care what he wanted to say. She only knew that she could not face him with any dignity.

Kirsty dropped into a lower gear and shot out to overtake two cars, only just getting back in before a lorry came hurtling up in the opposite direction. Normally that would have been enough to have her shaking with fright, but the need to escape was more to the front of her mind, and over the next few miles she took risks that she would never have taken at any other time.

Adam was taking no risks, and as she turned into the drive she knew she had left him behind. It would give her time to get into the house and he would not force his way to her there. But she was not halfway up the drive before he came in through the gates, and this time he accelerated after her with all the speed and power at his command.

When she stopped outside the front of the house he was tight in behind her, and she had not even got her door fully open before he was there, wrenching the door from her grasp and hauling her out of the car, fury on his face.

'You lunatic!' he snarled, his face white with rage. 'I've seen you almost kill yourself four times in the last few miles. It's a miracle you're still alive!'

'I have no wish to speak to you,' she told him shakily. It was pretty much impossible to take the stance she had intended because her legs were shaking, and not only because Adam was there. That mad drive had frightened her, and she could only agree with him that she was a lunatic. In any case, it hadn't done one bit of good.

'Then it would have been a damned sight safer simply to keep your lips tightly closed than to drive like a maniac!' he snapped. She knew all that, and she managed a small glare at him before she turned to the steps.

'Goodbye,' she said stiffly, but that was as far as she got. Adam grasped her arm again and swung her round.

'Oh, no, you don't!' he stated coldly. 'After having me on the edge of a heart attack for the last few miles, you're not just walking off. I want to talk to you.'

'We have nothing to say to each other,' Kirsty managed unevenly. 'I—I know I owe you an apology. I misjudged you for so long, and now I can only agree with you that it was a schoolgirl interpretation of things. I didn't even have the courage to confront you with it for three years. So, I'm sorry, Adam and—and now there's nothing more to be said.'

'*Really*?' he exclaimed sardonically. 'You think you can neatly tie off the ends with a few brief sentences? You think I chased all this way after you to hear you make that little speech?'

'If you didn't then I don't know why you came,' Kirsty murmured miserably. 'You—you never come here now. If you want to see my father then it's easy enough to see him at work, and you don't have to involve me in it.'

'You think you're not involved with me?' he asked tersely, and she looked down at her feet, avoiding his probing grey eyes.

'Not now. Not any more. You've got your own life, Adam and—and I've got mine. I'm glad the apartment has been such a success. At least it was one thing I could do for you. If your—your friend wants more doing, I'll do it. She only has to get in touch with me.'

His tight grip on her arm relaxed and she took the opportunity to pull away and turn again for the door, her escape.

'Kirsty!' he said deeply, but she didn't answer. She couldn't and when he caught her and pulled her back against the strong warmth of his body, Kirsty struggled frantically. She couldn't be close to him again, couldn't let him touch her except in anger, and now he was being gentle. Compassion would just about kill her.

'Let me go, Adam,' she begged piteously. 'You've made a new life and I'm not in it. Just let me go.'

His arms tightened and he bent his head to hers. 'Kirsty,' he murmured against her hair. 'Kirsty, forgive me.'

'Forgive you?' she whispered brokenly, turning to look up at him. 'There's nothing to forgive. I'm the one who needs forgiveness. All my life you took care of me and——'

'Only because I loved you,' he said unevenly. He turned her towards him, holding her almost cruelly tight, his face buried in her shining hair. 'I wanted to make you see what it had been like. I wanted to make you wait too, but I never meant you to be so hurt that you would risk your life to get away from me.'

'If you want,' Kirsty began, turning her face against the fabric of his jacket, fighting off the terrible urge to cling to him, 'if you want, I'll see the—the woman you're living with, and ask her how she wants the apartment altered.'

'If anybody ever lays a finger on that place they'll never get out of the door in one piece,' Adam told her fiercely, turning her pale face up to his. 'You did it for me. I'll never allow it to be altered.'

'But Selina said——'

'There is no woman, angel-face,' he said softly. 'I know what Selina said. It drifted back to my ears. It's the last time she'll have the chance to hurt you.' He cupped her face in his hands, threading his fingers in her hair. 'The only woman who has ever been in that apartment is you. The only woman who will ever be there is you.' He smiled into her eyes, his mouth twisting ruefully. 'I never did manage to get you out of my bloodstream,' he confessed gently. 'I tried, but you're too much a part of me.'

Kirsty looked up at him, her eyes searching his face, and he shrugged almost helplessly.

'Don't tell me I'm not in your life, Kirsty,' he begged softly. 'It's the only life I've ever had. It's the only place I want to be. If I'm not with you, where am I?'

'Adam!' Her green eyes were glowing, swimming with tears, and his fingers wiped the tears away before he gently kissed her eyes closed.

'Oh, love,' he murmured tenderly, and Kirsty wound her arms tightly round his neck, giving in to the urge to cling to him and never let go, and when she reached up and began to plant heated kisses all over his face Adam gave a shaken laugh and held her away, looking down at her with smiling grey eyes.

'Don't leave me again,' she pleaded distractedly, and he kissed her hard and fast.

'I never did leave you,' he reminded her. 'It's something I just can't do.' He sighed and turned her to the door, his arm around her waist. 'Let's go inside,' he suggested huskily. 'Standing here, looking at each other, is simply frustrating. Right now I'm wishing I still lived at the lodge. At least there we had a place of our own for a while.'

She knew what he meant. She didn't want to share Adam with anyone right now. They had so much to talk about, so many things to explain, and as soon as they got into the house her father would pounce on Adam and start talking.

He was just walking across the hall as they came through the door and he stopped for a minute, studying their slightly dishevelled appearance.

'What happened to you two?' he asked, and Adam laughed softly.

'Nothing unusual. A fight and a discussion.'

'Oh.' Her father lost interest and beckoned to Adam eagerly. 'Come into the study. I've just realised something about that latest deal.'

'Not yet,' Adam said firmly, making his way to the small sitting-room, taking Kirsty along with him and clearly expecting Donald to follow. 'First, I have something to say to you.'

Kirsty glanced at her father. His intrigued look was back and he came at once. She was intrigued herself. Adam was holding her wrist as if she would run off at the first opportunity, but she had no intention of doing that ever. She was singing inside, more happy than she had ever been, and as they all went into the room Adam shut the door firmly behind them and turned to her father.

'Donald,' he said clearly, 'I intend to marry Kirsty. I'm not *asking* either of you, because if either of you said no, I'd go completely out of my mind. I've waited long enough. Now I'm not waiting at all. As soon as I can arrange it you'll be giving Kirsty away, and I'll be standing there waiting to collect her. Don't argue, because I'm not listening!'

Kirsty's heart leapt with joy, and her father looked at her and began to laugh.

'Who's arguing?' he asked drily. 'I only have to look at her face. I can't imagine why you didn't say this years ago.'

'Neither can I,' Adam said grimly, his hand sliding from Kirsty's wrist to curl around hers possessively. 'Apparently, wisdom comes with age.'

'It took me a damned long time,' her father muttered wryly. 'Well,' he added happily, 'that takes care of dinner-time conversation.'

'I'll tell Mrs What's-her-name to set another place,' Kirsty said distractedly, and Adam grinned down at her. His thumb had been probing her palm erotically, making her knees weak, and he knew just how she felt.

'Jones,' her father reminded her as she made her escape. 'Easy enough to remember.'

Kirsty nodded, avoiding Adam's sensuous smoky gaze. Her cheeks were flushed and her heart was beating wildly. Over the last half-hour, her life had changed completely. She closed the door behind her and almost danced across the hall. Adam loved her still. He had always loved her and now he was going to marry her. She raced into the kitchen and stammered out the orders to the motherly woman who looked after them now. Then she hurried back to Adam, not wanting to miss even one minute of being with him.

'You'll stay the night?' Donald Sinclair asked as Mrs Jones served dinner, and Adam glanced at Kirsty, seeing the way her expression pleaded with him.

'Anything to have more time with Kirsty,' he said softly, his eyes devouring her as her father gave orders to the housekeeper to have the room that Adam usually used made ready.

They wanted to be alone but it was just not possible, and neither of them could deny her father the joy he was feeling at that moment.

'I've prayed for this for years,' he said quietly, raising his glass to toast them. 'It always seemed so right. I could never understand why you two parted for so long.'

'She was young,' Adam said softly, his eyes warmly on Kirsty. 'What does it matter, though? We're back together and that's the main thing.'

'I want to ask you something,' Donald said uneasily after a while. 'I know it's selfish, and if you both refuse I'll not be offended.'

'What is it, Daddy?' Kirsty's hand came to cover his. 'You know how we both care about you.'

'I know, I know,' he muttered. 'But what I want is asking too much, maybe.'

'Try us out,' Adam suggested with a laugh. 'Nothing is going to shock us unless you try to stop the wedding.'

'It's about Parbury Hall,' Donald said with the same unease. 'Kirsty has been away from here for a long time, and I know it was my fault for allowing Selina to drive her away. Now that she's back, though, I want to see more of her.' He looked up at Adam and then at Kirsty. 'When you're married, will you both live here? It's a big place,' he hurried on before they could reply, 'I know you'll want to be alone and we could have it altered, make a separate wing of the west side to give you a place of your own. I'd see you, though. Will you think about it?'

Kirsty's eyes met Adam's and she didn't need to say anything. Everything he was feeling was right there. This was their magical place, this was their past. That it could also be their present and their future was important to both of them.

'It will be yours one day,' her father pointed out anxiously, and Adam smiled across at Kirsty as he reached for her hand.

'We'll live here, Donald,' he said quietly, 'and neither of us wants anything altered. The place means too much to us. I can't see any reason why we shouldn't all be happy here, and, in any case, Kirsty and I have a very smart apartment in London if we want to escape for a day or two.'

'I've got a lot of time to make up at Parbury,' Kirsty told her father warmly. 'And who's going to order you about if I go?'

'Then that's my last worry over,' her father sighed happily. 'Now we can discuss this wedding.'

'How does it feel to be asked to share a house?' Adam murmured later, as her father went out for a minute. He pulled her down to the settee, close to him, and tilted her smiling face to his. 'Newly married couples like to be alone.'

'It's a big house,' Kirsty pointed out. 'We can hide in it with no trouble.'

'I used to consider that when you were seventeen,' Adam mused sensuously. 'I was crazy about you.'

'And I spoiled it all,' Kirsty said sadly. 'I stupidly threw it all away.'

'No regrets,' Adam ordered. 'It's only a small part of our lives. Anyway,' he added, kissing her urgently, 'I'm more crazy about you than ever now. Waiting adds a great desperation to feelings.'

Later, when the house was quiet, Kirsty lingered in her warm scented bath, her mind turning over the whole evening with a kind of delirious happiness. Adam was here. He was in this house and he loved her. It had been obvious all through the evening that he desperately wanted to be alone with her but he had never tried to get her away from the house. Her father had been happy and Adam would never do anything to change that.

She dried herself and slid into her nightie, her emotions too sweeping even to consider sleep. It was midnight, and Kirsty felt she would still be here, walking about, wide awake, when morning came. She was too happy, too restless to sleep, and her mind went back to another midnight, when she had been at the lodge with Adam, when she had willingly become part of him. She wondered if he was remembering that too, or if he was sleeping, waiting as she was for morning.

Kirsty reached for her silky négligé and slid her arms into it, not even giving herself time to think, and seconds later she was walking down the long, softly lit corridor that led to the room Adam always used when he stayed in the old house.

It was the first time she had ever taken the initiative, but she wanted to be with him so urgently that morning seemed to be years away. She didn't even know if he would be asleep, but as she came to his door Kirsty knocked softly, and then turned the knob, knowing now that he would never be annoyed with her.

The lights were on in his room, and as she stepped inside Adam stopped pacing about, and looked at her with the same quiet desperation she was feeling herself. His eyes moved over her hungrily and she closed the door behind her, leaning back against it.

'I couldn't even think about sleeping,' she whispered unsteadily, looking at him with shimmering eyes.

'Kirsty!' Adam was beside her at once, drawing her urgently into his arms, kissing her over and over, compelling, overwhelming caresses, that left her at the mercy of his fierce passion. He buried his face against the scented skin of her neck after a while, giving her time to breathe. 'If you hadn't come to me I would have been walking about all night. I just can't be away from you any more.' He gave a shuddering sigh and drew his head back to look down at her. 'Darling! Oh, my darling. I can't believe that we're safely together at last.'

'I—I suppose I shouldn't be here,' Kirsty managed shakily, 'but I wanted to be with you.'

'Did you?' His hands slid over her ribcage, finding the warmth of her breasts, desire flaring from his fingertips. 'Did you want to sleep with me, my love? Did you want to lie in my arms all night and belong to me again?'

Kirsty moaned softly, her head thrown back enticingly, and Adam's hands tightened on her hips as he pulled her closer, his lips searching her neck and moving lower. His hands held her against him and Kirsty's soft body surged to meet his, her legs too weak to hold her up.

'Oh, God! I want you,' Adam breathed raggedly. 'I'll never have enough of you. I'll never have you close enough.' His hands slid away her négligé and came impatiently to her nightie straps. 'Let me undress you, darling,' he murmured thickly. 'I want to see you again, to feel you against me.'

Kirsty's fingers were impatient too, tearing at the buttons of his shirt, and he pulled it over his head and tossed it to the floor as her nightie slid away to pool silkily at her feet. He looked down at her, consuming her with his eyes, and then he lifted her against him and Kirsty wound herself around him, pressing herself close to him as her arms tightened round his neck. He swung her into his arms and walked to the bed.

'You're not close enough,' he groaned, his head lifting from her breast as he shrugged out of the rest of his clothes. 'I want you now, sweetheart,' he gasped jaggedly. 'Don't let me hurt you.'

But he didn't hurt her, because Kirsty was heated by the same fire, her body welcoming him. She arched back,

unable to stop the wild cries that came from her throat.
Adam's possession sent her spiralling into shattering
fulfilment almost at once, and he held her tightly as they
splintered into the same delight.

It seemed like a blissful lifetime before Adam let her
go, and she rested her face against the damp skin of his
chest.

'I'm sorry,' he said thickly. 'I never intended to take
you like that. Now I feel like a barbarian.' He cradled
her head against him, his hands still restless on her
flushed skin. 'Did I hurt you?' His voice was almost
harsh, his heart thudding away against her, and Kirsty's
arms wrapped tightly around him.

She looked up at him with green seductive eyes, and
Adam's hands tightened on her, his own eyes flaring with
sensuous pleasure at the look on her face.

'I was fairly primitive myself,' she confessed, gasping
with regret when she noticed the lacerations her nails
had made on his shoulders. 'I hurt you!' she exclaimed,
and Adam looked sideways, seeing the damage, his wry
grin tantalising and slow.

'Just remember that the next time you tell me you're
not wild,' he said. 'And don't think you're escaping,'
he added softly, 'not after looking at me like that. Until
we're married, Donald can just get used to the idea that
you live with me.'

'I'll tell Mrs Jones in the morning,' Kirsty murmured
demurely, and then they were lying together, smiling into
each other's eyes, and Adam stroked his hand down her
body, his warm fingers coming back to fondle the rosy
tips of her breasts. His touch was possessive, and all the
wild feelings in Kirsty were soothed away. She was be-
witchingly submissive, irresistible, and Adam's eyes came
to hers as he felt her changed mood.

'If you knew how much I want you,' he breathed harshly, 'you would be scared.'

'The only thing that can scare me is if you stopped loving me.' Kirsty looked at him seriously, and his expression softened as he kissed her lips with aching tenderness.

'I never have stopped loving you,' he said quietly. 'I tried to, when I thought it was hopeless, but the thought of you never left my mind. Finally, I just let it overwhelm me and admitted to my fate.'

'Is that when you had the apartment redecorated?' Kirsty asked, suddenly understanding the despair that had been almost tangible as she had first gone with him there.

'Yes.' Adam rolled on to his back and curled her in his arms, pulling the sheets over them. 'A fit of blind frenzy, I suppose,' he confessed. 'There seemed to be no future. I was lashing out like an animal in pain. I wanted to roar violently and smash everything in sight.'

'Oh, Adam!' Kirsty clung to him, her hand stroking his face. 'Why didn't you tell me the truth years ago? I know I should never have doubted you, but I was so stupid. Why didn't you shout at me, and tell me all the things you knew about Selina?'

'It was not quite that easy,' Adam said seriously. 'In the first place, I had no idea why you were suddenly so cold, why you were avoiding me. Do you remember when I first ran you to ground at that flat? You told me you didn't like me any more. You said you had grown up.' He clutched her convulsively to him. 'I believed you. I thought your adolescent attachment to me had been just some youthful crush that was over.'

'I *always* loved you!' Kirsty insisted, pulling herself up to look down into his eyes. 'I thought there was Selina, and it hurt and hurt.'

'I know, my love. I know how much it hurt, and for how long, but I didn't know then.' He stroked her shining hair back from her face, looping it behind her ears. 'When I saw you at the opening of that boutique you looked so beautiful that it took my breath away, and still you tried to avoid me.'

'Without a lot of success,' Kirsty reminded him, blushing softly when he suddenly laughed.

'As a matter of fact,' he confessed, 'I was in a mood to strangle you. When you suddenly told me why you'd made me suffer for so long, I couldn't believe it. You were lucky to get off so lightly.'

'I didn't,' Kirsty protested. 'You humiliated me.'

'It was either that or make love to you right then. Somebody had to stop and it obviously wasn't going to be you, my angel.' He pulled her over him and cupped her face in his hands. 'I decided that I would never tell you the truth. I went off in a mad rage, and before I got over the rage Donald told me about Wentworth and I knew that I'd lost you anyway.'

'Told you?' Kirsty exclaimed. 'But there was nothing to tell. I just went out with Guy from time to time.'

'All the time, according to Donald. That was when I went crazy and had the apartment stripped out.' He sighed and looked at her seriously. 'Actually, I didn't want to live anywhere. The magic had slipped through my fingers. Parbury Hall was almost a torture because it reminded me of every little thing about you. I lived at the lodge for far longer than was necessary because I hoped you would come back, even for one evening.'

'Well, I did,' Kirsty soothed urgently, 'and I was terrified when I knew you were going to be here. I thought I couldn't face you.'

He pulled her down to him, kissing her passionately, and when she had escaped from this enchantment Kirsty lay contentedly against his shoulder and asked, 'Why did you make love to me at the lodge?'

'Because I couldn't help myself. After wanting you for years, you were there—soft and warm. We were really alone, for the first time ever. It was different from being at my apartment. The old magic was all around us, all the past, and you looked as you used to look—innocent, vulnerable. I just intended to hold you close, but it wasn't enough. It will never be enough.'

It wasn't enough then. Kirsty heard the ardent longing in his voice and turned to him willingly when he reached for her. It was still like a dream, and she looked up into his darkened eyes as he moved over her. He was so beloved, so familiar to her.

'Is it real?' she whispered, and he traced her lips with the tip of his tongue.

'It's real,' he assured her huskily. 'It's been real for years. You made me wait a long time, angel-face, and there's a lot of catching up to do.'

Later, as she lay warm and sleepily content in his arms, Kirsty asked about Selina. 'Did you have the proof in your safe?'

'I don't even have a safe of my own,' Adam laughed. 'And details of Selina's infidelity are not something I would want to keep in the office safe. The threat was enough.'

'Did you have someone following her from the first?' Kirsty wanted to know, interested in the intrigue.

'No. I saw her myself originally, and as time went on she became more and more sure of herself. I only needed a couple of photographs of them together, and they were easy to commission. Then I waited. When she rang the apartment she wanted me to sound out Donald for a divorce, but there was no mention of a man. She still thought it was a secret.'

'But when I heard you, a long time ago...'

'I don't even know what you heard,' Adam said softly, kissing the tip of her nose, 'but there were a few threats flying about that night. Selina knew how I felt about you and she didn't like the idea. She hinted that your father would be less than pleased if she told him. I retaliated about her infidelity, and at the time she felt so safe that she thought it was amusing. We both kept quiet for different reasons. My reason was to protect Donald, until he found out just what she was.' He turned to her urgently. 'I never thought it would be the cause of losing you.'

'I should have shouted at you and accused you then,' Kirsty murmured sadly, and he clasped her close, smiling against her skin.

'You never were the sort of person to shout, my sweet,' he reminded her, 'that ability grew as you got older.' He lifted his head and looked into her eyes. 'Let it go, Kirsty,' he begged softly. 'We're back together, right where we belong. And maybe it was a good thing.'

'How could it be, with both of us unhappy?' Kirsty demanded fiercely.

'You grew up,' he told her. 'You built a thriving business all by yourself.' He ran his hands over her seductively. 'You're a woman, not a seventeen-year-old angel I would be scared to make love to.'

'There is that,' Kirsty agreed, blushing at the look in his eyes.

'Then shall we forgive ourselves?' Adam asked tenderly, and she nodded, sinking into his arms, meeting his kiss with delight.

'It will soon be morning,' she sighed against his lips, and he trailed kisses over her face.

'Another day, another reason to be alive now the magic is back in my hands,' he said.

And Kirsty wound her arms tightly around him, clinging on to the magic that had always been there waiting, pouring all her love out to the man who had been in her life for so long and who would be in it forever.

'I love you,' she whispered ardently.

'I know,' he murmured against her lips. 'You always did. You just forgot for a while, but it's more real now than a teenage dream. Tomorrow we'll plan that wedding.'

'And tonight we'll just sleep,' Kirsty sighed.

'Later,' Adam said huskily, as his lips captured hers with such passion that Kirsty just drifted into rapture and forgot all about the time.

HARLEQUIN PRESENTS

HARLEQUIN PRESENTS
men you won't be able to resist
falling in love with...

HARLEQUIN PRESENTS
women who have feelings
just like your own...

HARLEQUIN PRESENTS
powerful passion in
exotic international settings...

HARLEQUIN PRESENTS
intense, dramatic stories that will keep you
turning to the very last page...

HARLEQUIN PRESENTS
The world's bestselling romance series!

◈ *Harlequin®* *Historical*

From rugged lawmen and
valiant knights to defiant heiresses
and spirited frontierswomen,
Harlequin Historicals will
capture your imagination with
their dramatic scope, passion
and adventure.

Harlequin Historicals…
they're too good to miss!

HARLEQUIN®

I N T R I G U E ®

We'll leave you breathless!

If you've been looking for thrilling tales of
contemporary passion and sensuous love stories
with taut, edge-of-the-seat suspense—
then you'll *love* **Harlequin Intrigue!**

Every month, you'll meet four new heroes
who are guaranteed to make your spine tingle
and your pulse pound. With them you'll enter
into the exciting world of Harlequin Intrigue—
where your life is on the line
and so is your heart!

THAT'S INTRIGUE—DYNAMIC
ROMANCE AT ITS BEST!

HARLEQUIN®

I N T R I G U E ®